Noah saw a dark fi
shadows and appro
high above her head. A warning cry burst
from his mouth as Noah ran toward her with a
speed he didn't realize he possessed.

Maggie glanced up and backpedaled from the assailant in time to avoid the first slash, but tripped over a piece of rough sidewalk and fell, landing on her back. When the figure stood over her and raised an arm to try again, she lashed out with a booted foot, catching the assailant on the knee. Noah heard a deep, guttural howl of pain.

He arrived in time to tackle the attacker, knocking the knife out of the big man's hand and across the sidewalk. Noah wrestled him to the ground and tried to pin him down, but the attacker got a hand free and punched Noah in the jaw. Noah's hold loosened as he fought the pain and dizziness and the big man pushed Noah off of him and staggered to his feet, limping into the shadows. Though Maggie called out for the man to stop, the attacker had already gotten away.

Books by Tina Ann Middleton

Nikki Dog
Love and Grace
Mistaken Target
Hidden Target

Tina Ann Middleton

Tina Ann Middleton has written poems, essays, and stories since childhood. A voracious reader, she likes to ask, "what if?" and then spin stories from there. Tina describes herself as having an active (and sometimes overactive) imagination.

She and her husband, Darran, have been happily married since 1981 and have two grown daughters. Tina works at a VA Medical Center as administrative support in a Primary Care clinic and greatly enjoys serving Veterans.

She is the author of four independently published books, *Nikki Dog, Love and Grace, Mistaken Target* and *Hidden Target.*

Follow Tina on:

https://www.facebook.com/tinaann.middleton

https://twitter.com/mid_tina

goodreads https://www.goodreads.com/author/
show/17729966.Tina_Middleton

The Forrestville Series
Book Three

Tina Ann Middleton

Shield
Of
Faith

Publishing

ISBN-13: 978-1-7348336-4-5

Copyright © 2022 by Tina Ann Middleton

Acknowledgments

This is the third book in the Forrestville series. While writing the first two, I realized that Maggie has her own story that needs to be told. I couldn't wait to write about her and her son Robert, but I absolutely could not have told Maggie's story without lots of help.

First, I want to thank my Heavenly Father for giving me the story and the words. I encourage all writers, ask God for help when you sit down to write. Thanks to God for providing the time to write during a week of leave from work and during a freak snowstorm in Northwest Louisiana. And, of course, the evenings when my husband took care of dinner and dishes so I could write.

That brings me to my husband, Darran, who gives me an incredible amount of support and encouragement. He's also my tea-bringer, cover designer, and all-around tech guy. Actually, he does everything except the writing; although he does help with that as well. Thank you, sweetheart for all the ways you support me in my writing.

Once again, our daughter, Kimberly, provided guidance regarding martial arts. It's kind of nice to have a third-degree black belt in the house who can answer my questions. She helps me make sure I keep things realistic.

Heaps of thanks and virtual chocolate to my beta readers Sharron Strawn, Tammie Benoit, and Virginia Disotell. Your input helps me make sure the story flows well and is enjoyable for the reader.

Thank you, Shannon Mack, for your valuable input regarding police and legal matters. Your help making sure the scenes are accurate and realistic is inestimable. If there are any errors, they are all my own.

I also want to thank the members of our local American Christian Fiction Writers (ACFW) group. Your encouragement and support mean so much to me. I love belonging to a group where we share our faith and a passion for books and writing.

There are many others who have helped in ways they might not even realize. Thank you to my friends and family who believe in me and support me by buying the books and encouraging me.

It's kind of like a recipe for a cake. Just as a baker takes flour, sugar, and eggs and puts them together to make a delicious cake, a writer needs to take all of the encouragement, support, and input and put them together to craft a book for the glory of God and the enjoyment of the readers.

God bless you all!

Tina Ann Middleton
May 2022

And forgive us our sins, for we also forgive everyone who is indebted to us.

Luke 11:14 (NKJV)

Chapter 1

"Surprise! Happy Birthday, Maggie!"

It seemed half of Forrestville had crammed into the party room at MaryAnn's Diner to celebrate her birthday. Maggie looked around at the sea of faces with a big grin on her face and tears in her eyes. These people were her friends. More than that, many of them were like family.

"Cut the cake, Mom."

Robert vibrated with excitement as he stood next to his mother. Maggie couldn't believe how much he'd grown in the past month. At twelve, his head came to just above her shoulder. Now he stood beside her, eager to dig into the luscious cake from The Sweet Shoppe.

Maggie handed him the knife.

"You cut the cake, son."

Robert's eyes widened with surprise.

"Really?"

"Sure, I think you'll do a superb job."

The boy's chest puffed out a bit. He bit his lip as he eased the knife through the creamy white frosting and into the rich chocolate layers. After cutting several generous pieces, he slid them onto paper plates and handed them to his mother, who passed them to the eager townspeople gathered around.

Esther and Stephen Abrams came to stand beside their police chief and friend. Stephen scowled at her when he saw her helping.

"Why are you serving the cake? You're the guest of honor."

Maggie grinned and shook her head as she handed a plate with a large piece on it to a teenage boy who began devouring the treat as soon as it was in his possession.

"Don't you remember? My duty is to 'serve and protect.'"

Stephen favored her with another scowl and took a firm grip on her arm, steering her toward a table and chair decorated and marked for her.

"Cute. Come on. You're going to sit in your special chair while *we* bring *you* a piece of *your* cake and some punch. Or would you prefer coffee?"

Maggie resisted for a few more minutes before she conceded to be led away from the table. She stopped beside a wooden chair festooned with crepe paper streamers and at least a dozen mylar balloons sporting varying birthday greetings.

"You've got to be kidding! This is my chair? How am I going to sit there without messing up the decorations?"

Stephen and Esther laughed and waved their hands in exaggerated motions toward the "throne." Maggie pushed aside a few strands of the streamers and arranged the balloons to float behind her, before she settled into the chair and watched with pride as Robert played host.

He seemed to soak up the attention he received from the surrounding group. She couldn't help remembering birthday parties for her son when he was only a toddler running around in diapers and t-shirts with cute sayings. Maggie smiled a little wistfully as she realized again that Robert was no longer a small child.

"Hey?"

She looked away from her son and caught Esther's knowing look.

"Yes?"

Esther motioned toward the cake and the eager boy handing out pieces.

"Robert sure is growing up."

Maggie nodded.

"Yeah, he is. It's hard to believe he's already twelve."

Stephen handed her a plate with an especially large piece of cake along with a steaming cup of MaryAnn's special brew coffee. He tapped her shoulder with his fist and winked at her.

"He's a good kid. I know you're proud of him."

Maggie watched Robert as he talked and joked with those around him. She smiled at the sight of him whispering in his best friend's ear and the two boys laughing at the joke.

"I am very proud of him."

The party wound down two hours later. Most of the townspeople who had only come to shake hands with Maggie, wish her a happy birthday, and sample the delicious cake left early. The group remaining in the party room were her closest friends.

Maggie felt a tug of regret as she looked around the room. It seemed everyone except her was part of a pair. Stephen and Esther sat hand-in-hand, her other hand cradling her baby bump. Jesse and Rachel sat nearby; his arm slung around her shoulders as they described their honeymoon in the Ozarks. David and Christy stood at the refreshment table, helping to box up the rest of the cake for Maggie to take home.

They were all couples. Maggie sighed. She couldn't help remembering a time when she was part of a couple. That was before everything fell apart, leaving her as a single mom who was trying her best to raise her son to be a godly, caring man. The hard times had worked to enrich the relationship between mother and son, however. They had a great relationship where both of them ensured they were truthful and open with each other.

Maggie felt a twinge of guilt. She had been *mostly* truthful with her son. But there were some things he didn't know; and she would do her best to make sure he never found out.

"Maggie Jones, Police Chief in Forrestville, Louisiana Breaks Up Drug Ring."

Micky threw the newspaper onto the dirty floor and snatched another one from a pile on the cluttered table, causing the pile to topple.

"Forrestville Police Chief Maggie Jones Captures Industrial Spy."

He tossed that one on top of the first and picked up a yellowed piece of newsprint with a photograph of a female police officer; her face serious under her police cap. Walking to a dartboard hanging on the back of a closet door, Micky stuck the picture onto the board with a pin. Hatred smoldered in his dark eyes as he gathered three darts in his hand, then stood back to glare at the photo.

A younger man sat on the tattered couch, listening as his companion ranted about the cop who had ruined his life. Although he kept a nonchalant appearance, Zach was quaking. Mickey sounded like he'd gone nuts! He wondered, not for the first time, why he hung around with the guy. Zach cringed as the older man vented his anger on the picture on the dartboard.

"Maggie Jones, you ruined my life!"

Thwack! The dart stuck just to the left of the pictured face.

Zach had no answer to the question of why he stayed, yet he felt reluctant to leave. Besides, this was his apartment, and he had worked hard to get what he had, little as it was. Mickey lived here, used his utilities, and ate his food, but contributed nothing. Yet, somehow Mickey had taken over his home and his life.

"Maggie Jones, I hate you."

Thwack! Another dart hit just below the picture, then clattered to the floor.

Zach guessed he allowed Mickey to stay because he was the only friend Zach had. Still, the ranting and talking about killing a cop were giving him the creeps. Maybe he'd just strike out on his own. Leave the apartment to Mickey and find another place far away from here.

Before he could get up and slide out of the apartment, the older man turned and pinned him with an icy gaze. It seemed Zach's body would not work to get up off the couch. After a long glare at the younger man, Micky turned toward the picture, malice etched in his craggy features.

He stalked forward with the last dart held like a spear and stuck it into the heart of the young officer in the newspaper picture.

"Maggie Jones, I'm going to kill you."

Micky stared at the picture with the dart dug deep into it. Suddenly, he turned and snatched up a battered duffel bag. He began stuffing dirty clothes into it.

Zach watched him with a bewildered expression on his face. He couldn't figure out what Mickey was up to, and he wasn't sure he wanted to know. When he got up from the couch and sidled toward the door, his friend interrupted him.

"Where you goin'?"

Zach started. Did Mickey know what he was thinking?

"I, uh, I thought I'd step outside for some fresh air."

The older man snorted and shook his head.

"We ain't got time for you to do no steppin'."

Zach watched him roll another dirty shirt and cram it into the bag.

"H…how come?"

His friend gave him a leering grin.

"We're goin' on a little vacation."

Somehow, Zach knew they weren't going for rest and recreation. He tried to make his voice sound nonchalant.

"Yeah? Where are we going?"

The older man shot a hateful glance at the newspaper picture fluttering on the dartboard.

"Forrestville, Louisiana. I want to pay a visit to an 'old friend' of mine."

Chapter 2

"Maggie, there's a call for you on line one from Emma Rogers. She sounds freaked out."

Maggie shook her head. How was it that whenever she tried to leave work early, or even on time, Emma Rogers always needed her? She set her jacket and purse on the desk and pushed the intercom button on the desk phone.

"Emma always sounds freaked out, Linda. What's bothering her this time?"

The receptionist chuckled.

"She won't tell me. I offered to send an officer, but she said this took your special touch."

Maggie sighed as she eased into her chair and picked up the phone. She was dead tired and still had things to do when she got home. But she was the police chief, and so was there to serve. Maggie took a deep breath, pasted on a smile, and punched the button on the phone to take the call.

"Hello Emma! What can I do for you?"

"Chief Jones!"

There was a gasp on the other end of the phone, then a loud, excited voice.

"There's a vicious dog wandering around the parking lot near the front of my store! My customers are afraid to get anywhere close to the door. Please, I need you to come deal with this animal. It's scaring my customers away!"

Maggie entertained a silent and hearty wish she had gotten away a few minutes earlier. Oh well, she had to make the best of it. She returned her attention to the frightened woman on the phone and injected a soothing tone into her voice.

"All right, Emma. Try to calm down. I'll be there in a few minutes."

"What should I do about the dog? Should I chase it away?"

"No, you called me to deal with it, and I'll take care of it when I get there. Stay inside and wait for me."

Maggie hung up and picked up her things from the desk, stopping to secure her gun and radio at her waist. She closed up her office and headed for the door, stopping at the reception desk on the way out.

Linda looked up with a mischievous grin.

"So, what's the big emergency this time?"

"She says there's a vicious dog outside the store. I'll check it out on the way home. It's been a long day."

Linda laughed.

"It's probably a Chihuahua."

"Hey, those can be pretty scary, you know."

The two women chuckled and Maggie turned toward the door at the same time her young son peeked in, his blue eyes hopeful.

"Hi mom! Can I ride home with you?"

His mother hesitated. She rarely liked to take Robert with her when she went on a call, especially with the possibility of a vicious dog loitering near the Handy Mart. She opened her mouth to tell him she had to handle a situation, and he needed to walk home. But when Maggie looked into her son's clear blue eyes, she relented. "Okay, son, you can ride home with me. But I have to make a stop first and I want you to stay in the car while I take care of it."

Robert's face lit up, and he agreed to do as his mother said as he dashed for the door. When they got into their small SUV, Maggie reminded him to buckle up. He rolled his eyes until she gave him "the look."

"Do you want to walk home instead?"

"No, ma'am. Sorry."

The boy hastened to put on his seat belt while Maggie put the SUV in gear.

When they pulled into the parking lot at the Handy Mart, Emma Rogers was standing near the door, tapping her foot and glancing at her watch with quick, nervous movements while also watching a dog that stood nearby sniffing the parked grocery carts. The animal was a young Rottweiler, barely out of puppyhood. Maggie's heart burned with indignation when she noticed the ribs showing on his thin frame. She hated when people dropped their dogs off instead of taking them to a shelter. Didn't they realize or care about the dangers to the animals or to other people? Maggie turned to Robert with a stern expression.

"I want you to stay here. We know nothing about this dog and it might be dangerous."

She didn't wait for his answer, but got out and began a slow approach toward the hungry canine. Maggie was so intent on the stray that she did not hear the car door open and close with a soft thud. As she reached toward the animal, a blur flashed past her and she saw her son dash to the dog, kneeling beside it and throwing his arms around its neck. The Rottweiler gave the boy a thorough face-washing with its tongue, its bobbed tail wagging its entire back end.

Maggie experienced several emotions in rapid succession - fear, relief, and anger at her son's blatant disobedience. She stood and fixed her son with an angry glare.

"Robert Blaine Jones! What did I tell you? And what have I told you about approaching a strange dog?"

The boy showed no repentance as he rubbed the dog's head and neck.

"But Mom, I knew he was friendly by his wagging tail. And the poor guy looked so lonely and like he needed a friend."

Maggie sighed as she pinched the bridge of her nose. She still had to swallow hard to overcome the horror that had flooded her when her son got up close to the big dog. Her voice showed a slight wobble as she reprimanded the boy.

"Robert, I've told you many times that you can't always tell by looking. Sometimes a wagging tail is not friendliness, it's a warning. Your disobedience could have gotten you injured or even killed."

The young Rottweiler whimpered at Maggie's stern tone and cowered behind his new friend. Her expression softened at the dog's reaction to her angry words. She had not intended to frighten the animal. When she opened her mouth to order her son back into the SUV, Emma's strident voice sounded behind her.

"Chief Jones, what are you going to do about that vicious animal? I can't believe you let your son even get near him!"

With a warning glance at Robert, Maggie stepped to the store owner's side to speak to her.

"It's okay, Emma. I'll take the dog with me until we can find its owner."

"But, aren't you going to put a muzzle on it or something? You know how Rottweilers are - they're savage beasts! There was a news story just last week about those dogs being used for fighting."

Now Maggie was the one who had to control the eye roll. Emma was always seeing a story "just last week" about something she wanted the police chief to investigate. But now that she had seen the dog, she knew it was little more than a puppy, and a good-natured one at that.

"Don't worry, Emma. I know how to handle dogs. I'll take care of this one."

Emma considered Maggie for a moment, then sniffed and nodded, her tight, worried expression relaxing a bit.

"I knew you were the one for this job, Maggie. That's why I asked for you specially. Thank you for coming to my rescue."

Maggie patted her on the shoulder and motioned for Robert to join her. He left the dog's side with reluctance and hurried to walk with her.

"Mom, we're not leaving him here, are we?"

"Robert, I want you to get in the car and stay there. You *will* mind me this time and when we get home, we're going to have a little talk about your disobedience and the consequences."

The boy opened his mouth to protest, but seemed to think better about it, and did as she told him. Maggie followed him and reached into the back for a muzzle and a leash.

"Mom, I don't think you'll need that muzzle. He's just a friendly pup."

"Son, it's standard procedure. We don't know for sure that he won't bite if he becomes frightened. The leash is to keep him from running away and perhaps getting hit by a car. It's for his safety as well as ours."

Maggie eased near the young dog, speaking in a soft voice to him. He cowered and backed away at first, until Maggie let him sniff her extended hand. Once he saw there was nothing to fear and approached her, Maggie slipped the leash around his neck. She drew him close to her and stroked his head and neck to soothe him. Then she showed him the muzzle and slid it onto him. Though he did not fight her, his eyes expressed anxiety. Maggie took another moment to stroke his back and give him time to adjust to the restraint.

Robert turned as far in the seat as he could to watch his mother load the dog into the back of the SUV. When she closed the hatch he hurried to turn to the front and buckle up. He understood he was in a lot of trouble for jumping out of the car after his mother had told him to stay put. But it was worth it. They were taking the dog home with them. Maybe he could persuade his mom to keep it. That would be great! He'd wanted a dog for a long time, but his mom always put him off, saying they might get one later. Robert sat and stared out the front windshield, dreaming about all the things he and his dog would do together.

Maggie got behind the wheel and sat for a moment, catching her breath. When she turned toward her son, Robert jumped in before she could speak.

"Mom, what are we going to do with him? We don't have an animal shelter in Forrestville. Please, don't take him to the pound in Shreveport. They'll put him to sleep. Please, can't we keep him?"

His mother considered as she put the SUV in gear and pulled out onto the street. As tired as she was, she didn't want to make the drive to Shreveport tonight. And she certainly didn't want to put the frightened dog in a shelter.

Maggie had received a bulletin that the Shreveport shelters had seen a large influx of dogs in the past few weeks and hated to add to the burden on the facilities. She looked into her son's pleading eyes and sighed.

Robert was going to get attached to this dog if they took him home. But she couldn't see any other way.

"All right, I guess we'll take him home with us."

Robert cheered, but stopped when she raised a hand to caution him.

"It's only until we find his owner, son. Don't get too attached."

"What if he doesn't have an owner? What if they abandoned him? Or abused him? What should we name him? We can't just call him 'Dog.'"

Maggie felt she might as well have talked to a stop sign.

"Robert, I told you, don't..."

She stopped and shook her head. I give up; she thought.

"What do you want to call him?"

When Robert sat for a few minutes without answering, Maggie thought he hadn't heard her. She stopped at a red light and glanced at him. He sat with his face scrunched in thought.

"Well, we could call him Elvis."

He shot a sly grin at her. He knew she enjoyed listening to Elvis CDs while doing housework.

Maggie chuckled at the suggestion.

"I don't think so."

"Hmm," Robert muttered. He looked in the rearview mirror where they could see the Rottweiler standing with his head over the back seat cushion. The boy's expression lit up with recognition.

"Bear!" he almost shouted. He beamed as if he had discovered something great.

"Bear?"

"Yeah! He looks like a bear, see?"

Maggie glanced at the young dog and nodded. She could see the resemblance.

"Okay, 'Bear' it is. At least until we find his owner."

"Or become his new owners."

Maggie almost didn't hear him. When what he said registered, her heart sank. What had she done by bringing this dog home?

The next day Maggie insisted Robert give the dog a bath.

"If that dog is going to stay in the house with us, he needs to smell a lot better than he does now."

In fact, Robert didn't mind bathing the dog. Even though Maggie had warned him not to get too attached, Robert and the young Rottweiler had already become fast friends. Robert had plans for all the fun things he and *his* dog would do together.

After the bath, Robert brushed the dog's coat until it shone. He dug in his sock drawer and pulled out a few dollars he saved from his allowance.

"Come on, Bear," he told his new friend. "Let's get you a nicer collar and leash."

The pair strolled to the dollar store in town. When they arrived, Robert looped the leash around a concrete post and commanded Bear to "stay." The big dog looked at him with a puzzled frown on his furry face, then lay down where he could watch the door.

Delighted, Robert gave him a pat on the head and rushed into the store. Fifteen minutes later, he emerged with a plastic bag in hand. He removed the collar that his mother had used and put it in the bag. He showed Bear a thick red collar which he buckled around the dog's neck. Last he attached a heavy-duty leash.

"Now we're ready for business!"

Robert reached into the bag again and pulled out a box of wrapped snack cakes and a bag of sugar-free hard candy.

"How about we visit Forrestville Rest Home and take some treats to the old people there?"

Bear wagged his back end and gave Robert a wet kiss on the cheek. The boy laughed as he wiped the slobber off his face. He gave the dog a brief scratch behind the ears, then motioned him forward.

"Let's go!"

Robert whistled as they walked toward the nursing home. He stopped to pick up a stick, which he used to run through a few karate moves. He searched the ground for a rock. When he found one he liked, he threw it in the air and tried to hit it with the stick. It didn't matter that he missed; he was just having fun.

As they neared the edge of town, a grizzled older man pushed past them, crowding Robert and Bear off of the sidewalk. Bear growled low in his throat, and Robert tightened his hold on the leash. The rude man shot a malicious glance their way.

"Stupid dog," the stranger muttered.

Robert turned and gave the man an indignant look, which went unnoticed. He watched as the man entered a store, then bent to talk to Bear.

"He's plain rude, isn't he, boy?"

Bear growled again and whined as he looked up at Robert for reassurance. The boy rubbed the dog's head as he sent another angry glance toward the door the man had entered. He stood in thought for a moment, then turned and grinned at his dog.

"You're right, Bear. We won't let him ruin our day. Come on, let's go visit those old people. I bet they'll like the goodies we brought."

When they arrived at the nursing home, a nurse's aide saw Robert enter with the big dog. She screeched as she scrambled to get behind the counter, pointing a trembling finger at Bear.

"You can't bring that dirty creature in here! Out!"

"He is *not* dirty! I gave him a bath this morning!"

"I don't care if you gave him a hundred baths. You cannot bring that big, dirty dog in this establishment!"

The boy and the aide faced each other, each refusing to back down while Bear sat and whimpered at the angry tones around him. At the sound of his dog's distress, Robert stroked his head and murmured reassuring words to him. He looked up at the woman with a determined scowl on his face.

"See what you've done? You scared my dog screeching like that!"

The aide opened her mouth to reply when a voice interrupted.

"Susan, what is the problem here?"

An older woman in a dress suit of red and black approached, her black dress boots clicking on the linoleum floor. Her air of command brought order as she addressed the nurse's aide.

"This boy is trying to bring a stinking dirty dog in here, Ms. Francis. And it, it's one of those big fighting dogs! What if it hurts a patient?"

The director of the nursing home turned her attention to Robert and Bear. Her impassive face softened when she looked down at them. A hint of a smile twitched ever so slightly at the corner of her mouth.

"Well?"

"Yes, ma'am. I thought the old people, I mean residents, would enjoy a treat and a chance to pet a dog. Isn't animal therapy good for old people? And Bear is not stinking, dirty, or a fighting dog. He's just a big friendly puppy. See how well he's sitting and waiting for us?"

Now the smile stretched across Ms. Francis' face. Robert thought it looked like she wanted to laugh, but not so much as a chuckle crossed her lips. She nodded at him while keeping her gaze on Bear.

"Yes, animal therapy is excellent for our residents, but our animals are trained and certified for therapy. What kind of treats did you have in mind? You know some of these residents are on special diets."

Robert showed her the wrapped snack cakes and the bag of hard candy he purchased at the dollar store. Bear sat next to him, looking around the waiting area and acting as if he was used to visiting nursing homes every day.

The director stared down at the two; her face thoughtful. After a moment's consideration, she nodded and clapped her hands once as she addressed the aide.

"Susan, I will allow the boy and the dog to visit."

When the aide opened her mouth to object, Ms. Francis held up a hand to stop her.

"It's all right. I believe this will be good for our patients."

She addressed Robert, her face stern.

"You may only visit with the patients in the area where I take you. Do not wander around the facility. I expect you and your dog to be on your best behavior. If there is any trouble, this will be your last visit here. Is that clear?"

Robert's eyes shone as he nodded and stuffed the snacks back inside the plastic bag.

"Yes ma'am! We'll be as good as gold."

A chuckle escaped from the nursing home director.

"Yes, I believe you will."

Zach swung the door to the small hunting cabin open and peered inside. Though the sun shone bright in the cloudless sky, the inside of the cabin was dark. He took a hesitant step forward, then stopped to fish his small penlight out of his backpack. The narrow beam provided a small amount of light, but it allowed him to see enough to get inside and pull back the piece of burlap that served as a curtain. That let in a little more sun.

Mickey grunted as he dropped his duffel bag onto the dirty floor, raising a small cloud of dust and leaves.

"Well, this is the place. I wonder if there's any grub left behind by the last bunch of hunters."

Zach shivered at the idea of eating anything left in the cabin. He didn't know how long it had been since anyone last used the dilapidated shack. He looked around the cramped space and sighed. It was even dirtier than his apartment in Shreveport. He wasn't all that worried about having everything in its place, but he did like his floors and bed to be clean. He looked around for a broom and found one behind the door, which he grabbed and started sweeping.

Mickey swore at him and tore the broom out of his hands, throwing it across the room.

"Don't be doin' no cleanin' while I'm in here! I don't want all that dust up my nose!"

Zach stared at him, his eyes wide with disbelief.

"But, Mick..."

"Don't 'but' me! You can clean when I ain't here."

"Where are you going?"

"Never you mind. What you don't know, you can't blab to someone else. Now, you listen to me. You stay here at the cabin. I'll do the scoutin' for food and such."

Zach wondered what "and such" included. Mickey had

planned this trip because he wanted to get even with the cop he blamed for ruining his life. Zach believed Mickey had ruined his own life, but he knew better than to voice that thought.

Mickey gave him a hard stare, and Zach realized he had missed something Mickey said. When he shrugged in apology, Mickey swore at him again.

"Pay attention, you moron! I said don't let anyone in the cabin or even near it. If some hunter shows up, tell him the place is taken."

"What if it's the hunter the cabin belongs to?"

"Are you stupid or somethin'? Why would this old pile of wood belong to someone? It's about to fall over!"

Zach wanted to ask why a hunter would want to use it, but one look at Mickey's threatening expression shut his mouth. He realized Mickey had only brought him along to watch their stuff while he was looking for a chance to hurt the cop. The thought that Mickey would carry out his threat terrified Zach. If Mickey killed the cop, and they were caught, Zach could be charged as an accessory to murder, and he would go back to prison for a very long time.

Was his "friendship" with Mickey worth it?

Chapter 3

Noah settled into his brown leather recliner and reached for the large mug of coffee sitting on the small table next to him. He paused and took a deep, appreciative sniff of the fragrant brew before sipping it. After he set the coffee on a coaster he picked up the Shreveport newspaper and folded it so he could read it more comfortably.

Most of the time he read the news on his computer, but now and then Noah liked the feel of the paper in his hands and the rustling of its pages as he turned them to read. Lately he had been so busy with his job at Sinclair Accounting, he hadn't had time to read the news - on the computer or in print.

Noah scanned the headlines on the front page, stopping to read a story that interested him. When he turned the page his heart seized.

"Forrestville Police Chief Maggie Jones Captures Industrial Spy."

Maggie!

A wave of shame and regret swamped him, and the coffee churned in his stomach. After their divorce almost 13 years earlier, he had not been in contact with her. She had told him in definite terms to stay away from her. The feelings of hurt, anger, and betrayal at her desertion caused him to comply without argument.

But now, things were different. He was different. Yet, even knowing how God had forgiven and changed him, Noah felt unsure the differences were enough. His eyes focused on the picture of his ex-wife and took in the details of her face. He read the entire story, then went back to the beginning and read it again, then again.

"Yo, earth to Noah!"

Noah started and looked up from the paper in his hands into the eyes of his roommate, Cyrus Wilkinson, also known as Cy. His friend's eyes were full of concern.

"Hey, man, you okay? You look like you're going to be sick."

Noah folded the paper so that Maggie's picture was on top and showed it to Cy.

"Who's that?"

"My ex-wife."

"Your ex-wife is a cop? Interesting."

When Noah didn't elaborate, Cyrus raised an eyebrow at him.

"Okay, there's something more here. C'mon, spill it."

Noah took a deep breath.

"You know how I'm supposed to make amends with everyone I hurt while I was drunk and on drugs?"

Cy nodded, his posture inviting Noah to continue.

"She's the most important one I need to make amends with. But, I haven't. It's too hard."

"Why?"

Noah started.

"Why what?"

"Why is it too hard?"

Noah got up and started pacing around the room, trying to find the words to explain how badly he had hurt the woman he loved.

"Because when we divorced, she told me she never wanted to see me or even hear from me again. If you'll notice the headline, she didn't even want to keep my name. Jones is her maiden name."

Cy reached for the paper, his eyes wide with astonishment.

"Wait! Let me see that picture again. Did you say her name is Maggie Jones?"

Noah handed his friend the newspaper, his expression confused when Cy grinned at the picture.

"Cy, what are you grinning about?"

"That's the cop who arrested me the last time. Her testimony sent me to prison."

"Okay, and that's a good thing?"

A booming laugh burst out of the big man.

"I owe her a huge debt of thanks. I met the Lord Jesus while I was in prison. Now I'm free!"

He sobered as he took in Noah's despondent attitude.

"You owe her a debt too, don't you? Tell me again why you haven't made amends with her."

Noah let out a frustrated sigh.

"The last time she saw me was at a drug bust. I was drunk and strung out, and she watched as they put handcuffs on me. It only reinforced why she left me."

Noah ran his hand through his hair and let out a low groan.

"Every day the regret and shame wrap around me like, like an octopus! I know God forgave me, but I still live with the consequences. The worst is remembering how much I hurt Maggie."

His friend stopped him with a heavy hand on his shoulder. Cy was his mentor, as well as his roommate.

"Noah, you will not experience any peace until you resolve this. Go to this little town and talk to her."

"But she doesn't want to see me!"

"Make the effort anyway. Remember, you do the right thing…"

"Right, and leave the results up to God."

Noah turned and moved toward his bedroom.

"I guess I better pack and call Mr. Sinclair to tell him I have to leave for a while. Maybe he'll let me work remotely on the Stanley project."

"You want me to come with you?"

Noah shook his head, grateful that Cy had offered.

"No, I think this is something I need to handle alone."

Cy walked over and got right in front of him, stopping his friend's progress into the bedroom and holding Noah's gaze with his own.

"Don't be too proud to accept help, Noah. That regret and shame you were talking about can lead you to make foolish choices."

Noah considered for a moment before nodding.

"If I get in a jam, I'll call you. This isn't pride, Cy. I just have a sense this is something that no one else can do for me. Thanks for the offer, though."

As Noah grabbed his suitcase and filled it, Cy eased down on the couch, his brows drawn in concentration. He remembered the pretty young cop who arrested him and knew her to be a strong and determined woman. Cy could see this was a very serious situation for his friend and his intuition told him Noah was going to need some backup.

He would pray about it and ask for God's direction.

Noah eased up on the accelerator as he drove past a sign welcoming him to Forrestville. He took advantage of a red light to glance around and find the police station.

When the light changed, he pulled into a parking space near the station and turned off his car.

He sat and stared at the station, fighting the attack of nerves that caused a fine tremor throughout his body. It was not because he was remembering the many times he spent in a jail cell after a binge. No, he was dreading who he needed to meet and talk with.

Over the past several years, Noah had realized just how much he must have hurt Maggie. When they had married, they were young and very much in love. He promised to love, honor, and cherish her. Instead, he allowed his addictions to cause him to shut her out. At the end, he had even tried to physically abuse her. Though she had defended herself, that had been the push Maggie needed to leave him.

Noah got out of his car and closed the door, his thoughts far away as he locked the vehicle and pocketed the keys. He stopped at the curb to control the shaking in his legs, then moved to confront his past. It was time to make amends for all the hurt he had caused.

The receptionist at the front desk looked up from her computer when Noah entered the police station. She paused her typing to give him her attention as he approached the desk.

"Can I help you, sir?"

Noah pasted on a polite smile and asked for directions to the police chief's office.

"Do you have an appointment with her?"

"No, but she knows me. I'm an old friend of hers."

The young lady paused, as if uncertain, then pointed down the hall.

"First door on the left."

Noah thanked her and moved to the office. He knocked and eased the door open when a voice said, "Come in."

The sight of his ex-wife after all these years was a shock to his system. He had forgotten how beautiful she was. The satiny blond hair that used to flow over her shoulders, Maggie now wore pulled into a tidy and efficient braid. Her smooth skin had a few fine lines, but her eyes still had the beautiful blue color that had so entranced him when they first met.

Maggie felt her guest staring and looked up from her work. At first, she did not recognize the man in her office. His short, dark brown hair and the dimple in his cheek seemed familiar. The moss green eyes held a wealth of sadness and regret. She gave him a puzzled look for a moment before recognition hit. Noah! Fear and rage rushed through her at the sight of him.

"What are you doing here?" she demanded, her hand resting on her Glock. "I thought you were in prison."

Noah's eyes followed the hand on the gun for a moment, then came to rest on Maggie. She had always loved those green eyes, but she hardened her heart. She believed if Noah was here; it was for nothing good.

Noah looked down for a moment, composing himself. This was harder than he had realized it would be. Finally, he raised his eyes, his heart sinking when he saw her hostile gaze.

"I went to trial and pleaded guilty, but the judge sentenced me to rehab. I've been clean for over five years. Maggie, part of my rehab is to make amends to the people I have hurt. I realize I hurt you the most and I ..."

"There is nothing you can do to make amends to me!"

Maggie stood and picked up the pistol, giving Noah a meaningful look as she placed the weapon in its holster on her belt. She regarded him for a moment, then after a quick glance at the clock on the wall, seemed to relent.

"I appreciate that you tried, Noah, and I'm glad you got your life straightened out. Thanks for coming by. I'm really busy now, so I will have to ask you to leave."

She moved around the desk as if in a hurry to usher him out of the office, her eyes wide with fear. Noah wondered why she seemed afraid. After all, they were in a station full of police officers and she had just put a pistol in her belt. He, on the other hand, carried no weapons.

"Hi Mom! Guess what?!"

A young boy bounced into the station, his blue eyes dancing with excitement. At the sight of the child, all the breath in Noah's body left him. The boy's brown hair was the same shade as his own. The dimple in the boy's right cheek matched the one Noah saw in the mirror every day. His head spun so that he hardly heard the conversation between the boy and his mother.

"Sensei Kennedy says I'm ready to study for my black belt! Will you help me get ready?"

"Of course I will, son. I'm incredibly proud of you. Let's talk about it at home, okay?"

Noah watched Maggie as she tried to get the boy out of the station and away from him. He sent her a look that stated he could see what she was doing and that he recognized who that child was. Maggie got the message, and her shoulders sagged slightly.

"Hi, I'm Robert."

The boy stood in front of him with his hand extended. Maggie groaned and moved to steer him away, but Noah grinned at Robert.

"Hi, Robert. My name is Noah Jameson. I heard you say you're ready to study for your black belt. What discipline are you studying?"

"We study several, but I'm getting my black belt in Isshynru karate."

"Wow, that's pretty impressive that a young man like you is already going to be a black belt."

"Well, it's actually a junior black belt, but it's still pretty advanced."

Maggie stepped between them and turned Robert toward the front door.

"Robert, remember what I told you about introducing yourself to people at the station? Now, it is time for you to go home and get your schoolwork and chores done."

There was no mistaking the stern tone in Maggie's voice.

"Okay, Mom, I'll go now. I just wanted to tell you about my black belt. Bye, Mr. Jameson, it was nice to meet you."

As Robert exited the station door, Maggie waved Noah toward her office.

"I think we may have a little more to talk about, after all."

Noah followed her and took the chair she offered, his shaky legs relieved at the opportunity to sit. He felt hot and cold all over.

"Is, is that ..?"

"Yes, that's the child I was carrying when we divorced. Do you remember the terms of our divorce?"

At her bitter words, Noah slumped in the chair. He remembered.

"I don't want you around him."

"But, Maggie, I'm not that man anymore. I've been clean for over five years. I even have a career as an accountant."

"That's all very good for you. I'm glad to hear it. But I still don't want to have anything to do with you and I don't want you around Robert."

Noah stood and paced around the small office. He was trying so hard, but she wouldn't budge. In his frustration, the words flew out of his mouth before he could stop them.

"I thought you were a Christian! Aren't Christians supposed to forgive?"

He knew the words were a mistake as soon as he said them. Maggie stood and slammed her hands on the desk, jarring the papers scattered across the top.

"Don't you dare try to use my faith as a weapon to get what you want! You wanted nothing to do with God during our marriage. Don't use Him now!"

She sat again, and glared at him.

"Now, get out."

Noah understood he had messed up and tears pricked the back of his eyes. He bowed his head and offered a desperate prayer.

"What do I do now, Lord? How do I fix this?"

His words were inaudible, but he meant them with all his heart. A gentle stirring moved in his heart as God convicted him of his pride. Noah stepped back and took a deep breath.

"Maggie, you're right. I'm sorry I said that."

He lifted his head and looked into her eyes.

"Actually, I came to Christ five years ago. The rehab facility the judge sent me to is a private, faith-based group of men who have been where I was and they hold me accountable. In fact, my sponsor is the one who told me I needed to come talk to you. Please, let me start over."

Maggie gave him a stony stare. At least she's not throwing me out, Noah thought.

"I understand I hurt you terribly during those last two years of our marriage. There are no excuses for what I did."

"You got that right," she muttered.

Noah swallowed and continued.

"An apology can never be enough, but it is a start. So, here it is. I am sorrier than you'll ever know for how much I hurt you and the things I did. I was a cold, abusive, selfish jerk and I know I don't deserve your forgiveness. The shame and regret for what I did to you will stay with me for the rest of my life, but I hope one day you can forgive me."

Maggie scrutinized him for a minute, her expression skeptical. As much as he had hurt her, Noah knew he would have to *show* her he had changed. Her next words gave him a small amount of hope.

"I accept your apology. I'm glad you got some help and seem to be doing well."

Noah noticed she did not say she forgave him, just that she accepted his apology. He decided to push things a little further.

"May I please have the chance to get to know Robert?"

When Maggie fidgeted with her pen on her blotter, Noah felt uneasy. Why was she avoiding looking at him now?

"I'll understand if you want to check me out first."

"Oh, I will. But, that's not the fundamental problem."

"What is, then?"

Maggie looked up at him and sighed.

"Robert thinks his father is dead."

"Wait, what? Why does he think his father is dead?"

Maggie met his gaze, her own expression reflecting the hurt of years past.

"Do you remember the day I told you I was pregnant?"

The memories almost overwhelmed Maggie as she thought about that day.

Her hand trembled as she held the home pregnancy test and stared at the two stripes. Positive! It was positive! Maggie snatched up her purse and hurried for the door. She wouldn't tell Noah until the doctor confirmed what the home pregnancy test told her. The room tilted and she had to slow down and grab the door frame for a few seconds until the dizziness and queasiness passed.

When Maggie returned from her doctor's office, she was bursting with the news. She was pregnant! They were finally going to have the baby they'd been praying for.

She opened the door and saw Noah sprawled on the couch, swigging a bottle of beer and munching on potato chips. A quick glance at the clock showed he was home about two hours early. He had been doing that a lot–arriving at work late and coming home early.

Maggie determined she would let nothing ruin her wonderful news, not even irritation toward her husband. She couldn't wait to tell him he was going to be a daddy! Maybe that would help settle him down from the partying and drinking.

Noah gave her an indifferent glance, then returned his gaze to the television.

"Where've you been? Shopping on your day off?"

Maggie turned off the television and stood in front of her husband. She set down the bouquet of pink and blue carnations and stood holding the balloons while her eyes shimmered with tears of joy.

"I have wonderful news!"

Noah sat up and eyed her, his expression wary.

Maggie clasped her hands over her racing heart, the

strings from the balloons dangling in front of her. Somehow, she had not pictured telling him like this. She had imagined him taking her hand and holding her close as she shared the news that they were going to be a family.

The reality, however, was that he barely showed any interest. He just seemed impatient at the interruption.

"Well? What's your news? I'd like to get back to my show."

"We're pregnant! I mean, I'm pregnant! We're going to have a baby!"

Noah stared at her for a minute, then shook his head.

"This is not a good time for us to start a family," he told her.

Maggie's stomach churned in disbelief. They had been trying for seven years. What did he mean, it was not a good time?

"What are you talking about?"

She choked on the words.

"We've been trying..."

"Yeah, yeah, I know."

Noah stood up and came to stand beside her. He laid his hand on her shoulder and turned her to face him. She searched his eyes for the warmth and tenderness that used to shine in them. Now his green eyes were flat and cold.

"Look," he continued. "A baby would just slow us down. We have lots of stuff we want to do that we can't do with a kid at home."

Maggie jerked away from him.

*"You mean **you** have lots of things to do, like partying and drinking. Noah, we've already started a family and I'm about six weeks along."*

He moved back to the couch and plopped down onto the cushions. He picked up the remote and gave her an indifferent glance.

"You'll need to get an abortion."

Maggie stared at him in horror. How could he even think about aborting their child?

"I am NOT getting an abortion! Noah, I can't believe you are saying these things. You wanted a baby as much as I did."

Maggie was crying now, but Noah didn't even seem sorry he'd upset her. He just turned on the television and picked up his beer bottle. After taking a long swig and wiping his mouth with the back of his hand, he looked up at her.

"I'm not ready to be a father. Get rid of it."

Noah stared out her office window, lost in the hazy recollection of that day. When his wife told him about the baby, his only response had been something so cold and hateful it seemed to belong to someone else-not him.

The memory hurt him as he wondered again how he could have been so selfish and uncaring. Of course, the answer was that he had allowed alcohol and drugs to master him and to become his gods.

Maggie sat watching him, her eyes seeming to dare him to contradict her.

"I'm not that man anymore."

"So you say," she shot back. "But I need proof, not empty words. Until then, you will come nowhere near my son unless I am with him. You got that?"

Noah had to swallow hard to keep from saying the bitter words on the tip of his tongue. He saw he needed to walk carefully and watch what he said if he wanted any chance of getting to know Robert. When he felt he could answer her, he nodded his head once.

"Understood."

Chapter 4

Noah stumbled past the storefronts with his head down and tears blurring his eyes. He didn't even notice the people passing by him. He was only aware of the fact that he had a son, and Maggie had told the boy his father was dead. How could he build a relationship with his child?

He sighed as the belief rose from within that Maggie would never let him be a father to Robert. He couldn't blame her. If he was in her place, he wouldn't allow someone he believed used drugs or alcohol to come anywhere near his son.

But he wasn't that man anymore! God had changed him. How could he prove to Maggie he was a different man now?

A door opened just ahead of him and as he caught a whiff of beer, old desires stirred within him. Noah remembered how it felt to hide from life in a haze of intoxication. His heart hurt and suddenly a beer seemed like the most desirable thing in the world.

Noah stood in front of the Pot O' Gold bar and struggled with his old life. He wanted a beer, but he didn't want to give up the freedom and new life he had found in Christ. He bowed his head and prayed, "God, I need Your help now." That was all.

Then he realized he was free, and he didn't need or want to hide inside intoxication anymore.

Just as he turned to walk away, he heard a voice behind him.

"I told you God would help you, didn't I?"

Noah turned and saw Cy standing behind him with a huge grin on his face. He laughed out loud and grabbed the big man's hand for a heartfelt shake.

"Cy! What are you doing here, man?"

"Watching you resist the lure of the devil, it looks like."

"Well, you showed up just in time. I know I told you I could do this on my own, but I am glad to see you because I realize I need help."

"Hey, brother, that's what I'm here for, so tell me what's going on."

Noah told Cy about his meeting with Maggie, and about seeing Robert for the first time. He hung his head in shame as he recounted the story of the day she told him she was pregnant.

Cy listened without comment until Noah finished, his face serious.

"Let's pray about it right now."

Noah nodded and bowed his head as his friend prayed right in front of the town's bar.

"Lord, You see my brother here is hurting. He knows he did wrong, and he has confessed and repented of those sins. Though we understand You forgive when we confess, we also recognize there are often consequences of those sins and Noah is experiencing those consequences now. Please give him strength and wisdom. Help him resist the arrows of temptation our enemy is throwing at him. In Jesus' name, amen."

"Thanks, man. That's what I like about your

prayers–they're short, sweet, and to the point."

"Let's get away from this source of temptation now."

Cyrus sniffed the air and turned toward MaryAnn's Diner.

"I think I smell the aroma of fresh apple pie and coffee coming from that diner."

Maggie strode down the sidewalk on her way to the local dollar store, thinking about the few items she needed to pick up before she went back to her desk to finish up and go home. She stopped in dismay when she noticed Noah standing in front of the Pot O' Gold. It was obvious he was watching the door and considering going in.

"So much for not having drunk in five years."

She sighed, surprised at the disappointment that filled her. She had hoped what he told her was true, but her eyes were telling her a different story now. When she saw a big man covered in tattoos stop and talk to him, Maggie thought for a moment, realizing the guy looked familiar. She remembered a drug raid, right after she joined the Shreveport Narcotics division, where she had arrested someone who looked a lot like him. Disappointment transformed into fiery anger.

"He's still hanging out with druggies and going into bars! No way am I letting him near Robert!"

Maggie seethed at the thought that Noah had tried to scam her into thinking he had changed, and she had almost believed him. It didn't occur to Maggie that he had no reason to find her and scam her. All she could see was that he was still hanging out with the same crowd.

She turned away in disgust and continued down the sidewalk. A strong unease rippled up her spine, like the sensation of being watched. Maggie stopped as if to retie her shoe and took a slow look around her. A young couple with a young child strolled by, looking in store windows. Over by the hardware store, several elderly men sat on benches and swapped tall tales. Nothing seemed out of the ordinary.

A blur of movement near the alley caught her attention, and Maggie stood to study the area. She glimpsed a man with unsightly stubble on his chin and a fierce glare directed toward her. He turned and disappeared into the alley.

With a sense that she had seen this man before, Maggie followed him down the alley, her hand resting on her pistol. She didn't want to scare an innocent bystander by having the gun drawn, but she wanted to be ready.

Maggie stopped in the middle of the alley and swept the area with her gaze. The stranger had disappeared, and the alley seemed deserted.

"Hello?" she called out. "Sir? Can I help you?"

All she heard was the sudden yowling from one of the stray cats that hung out in the area. Maggie rolled her eyes, though she couldn't help a sense of relief. The man was probably long gone, but she needed to find the cat and deal with it before business owners started calling the station to complain about the noise.

Just as Maggie stepped near a tall dumpster, a heavy figure in a black ski mask moved into her path, holding a cat in a meaty hand. Before Maggie could react, the attacker threw the cat in her face. The frightened animal landed on Maggie's neck and slid down her front, leaving several long scratches in its wake.

Maggie moved fast and grabbed the animal to stop its fall. As she stood with the trembling cat in her hands,

Maggie looked up in time to gaze into the glittering, hate-filled eyes of the figure in black, who had a knife and was moving toward her. A slight tremor ran through her at the realization that with her hands full with the frightened cat, she could not get to her Glock.

The dark figure raised the knife but stopped when voices came from a door opening into the alley. The would-be attacker turned and disappeared behind the dumpster. A moment later she heard the door close and footsteps coming behind her. She whirled to find Mindy Wallace, the owner of The Sweet Shoppe, watching her with a concerned expression.

"Chief Jones? What are you - Oh, you found the cat making all the noise. That was fast! I just called the station."

Maggie sagged with relief. She leaned against the brick wall and stroked the little cat she still held. The animal was a half-grown gray tabby with white feet and belly hiding underneath all the dirt on the matted fur.

"Chief Jones? Maggie? Are you okay? Your face is kind of pale. Did the cat hurt you? Oh my, those scratches are awful! You need to have your doctor check those out."

Maggie met the concerned gaze of the bakery owner.

"I'm fine, Mindy. Listen, I want you to be sure you keep your door to this alley locked, okay?"

"Sure, why?"

"I've seen several strangers in town. Until I find out who they are and what they're doing here, I'd rather we all play it safe."

Mindy looked over her shoulder, then back at Maggie with such a worried expression that Maggie experienced a twinge of guilt for scaring her. She hastened to explain.

"It's standard security precautions. I just want to make sure everyone is safe."

"Well, if you say so. I guess I'll go back inside and take care of some ginger cookies in the oven."

Maggie tried to lighten the mood, though her senses were still on overdrive from the attack.

"Mmm, is that what I'm smelling? I certainly don't want to keep you from those! In fact, I might have to stop in later to sample a couple."

After the bakery owner returned to her cookies, Maggie gave the alley one last sweep. As far as she could tell, she was the only one there. She shuddered as she thought about the attack and what might have happened if Mindy had not stepped out when she did.

Maggie turned her attention to the purring animal she held snuggled in her arm.

"Come on, little one. I can't leave you out here to starve."

She looked over her shoulder at the back door to Linda's Sweet Shoppe, then back at the kitten.

"How about I name you Cookie since a bakery owner rescued us?"

The kitten looked into her face with big green eyes and continued its purring. Maggie held it up to eye level and sighed, though she had to smile at the sight of the little animal.

"It looks like I now have a cat."

"Robert? Robert, I'm home! Come help me bring in the groceries!"

Maggie juggled her purse, the cat carrier, and a bag of kitty litter; finally dumping the purse and kitty litter on the floor so she could more carefully set down the crate.

She peered down the hall, smiling as her son stuck his head out of his bedroom door.

"Come on, kiddo, I need your help."

When Robert entered the room with Bear at his side, the Rottweiler noticed the carrier with the mewing kitten a couple of seconds before the boy did and trotted over to investigate. Robert's eyes widened as he took in the carrier and kitty litter. He hurried to his mother's side and tried to peek at the noisy animal.

"Mom? Is that a kitten?"

Maggie understood his surprise and laughed when she thought about their situation. They had gone from having no pets to taking in a Rottweiler whose owner she was no closer to finding and now adopting a stray cat. She eased Bear out of the way with her foot, unlatched the carrier and pulled out the now-clean kitten, which she handed to Robert.

"Yes, son, that is a kitten. Her name is Cookie, and I rescued her from an alley downtown. It's a long story, though, and we have a lot of groceries to put away. You can take a minute to get acquainted; then put her back in the carrier and come help me, okay?"

The boy sat on the couch, cradling the young cat and stroking her silky fur. Cookie stared up at him for a minute before she started purring. Robert grinned with delight. She liked him!

Bear nosed the little cat, his expression uncertain, so Robert reached with his free hand to rub the dog's forehead.

"Don't worry, big guy. You're still my buddy. Cookie's a part of our family now, though, so, you gotta help Mom and me take care of her."

Bear gave a slow wag of his back end and slurped

his tongue over the kitten's head. Robert laughed as he placed her back in the carrier.

"Come on, boy. We need to help Mom."

Chapter 5

As Noah and Cy entered MaryAnn's Diner, Noah inhaled the delicious aromas hanging in the air. The tantalizing smells of coffee, fried chicken, and homemade bread made his stomach rumble and reminded him he had skipped breakfast.

Out of the corner of his eye he could see his friend's eyes widen at the sight of the pastries on the counter. Cy had an incredible capacity for food, especially sweets. From the delighted expression on his friend's face Noah had a feeling the restaurant would make a tidy sum just from Cy's lunch order.

A server approached and guided them to a table, where she handed them each a menu and took their drink orders. After she left, the two men looked around the old-fashioned diner with interest.

Cy turned his attention to Noah, his dark eyes filled with compassion.

"You doing okay?"

Noah took in a deep breath. He was full of gratitude that God had taken away his desire to have a beer, but he was even more thankful for the man sitting at the table with him. Cy was more than his sponsor and friend. He was his mentor and brother in Christ.

"Yeah, I am. You have no idea how glad I was to see you. God took away my desire for a drink, but I still needed support so your arrival was timely."

"Yes, you mentioned that several times. I was afraid you would think I was meddling when I showed up right behind you after you told me you wanted to handle your situation alone. But I felt in my heart that God wanted me here to help you."

Noah smiled and bumped his friend's shoulder with his fist.

"Well, you are meddling, but that's okay. I think I might need someone to meddle at this point."

"Hey, man, you know I'm here for you and I'll do whatever I can to help."

Both men turned their attention to their menus, and each decided on a burger and fries. When Cy also ordered a large milkshake and a piece each of cherry and apple pie with ice cream, Noah raised a brow at him.

"Aren't you supposed to be cutting back on sweets and carbs?"

"Now who's meddling?"

When their meal arrived, the two men bowed their heads for a silent blessing, then dug in. Noah got a kick out of watching Cy enjoy his dessert as the big man even scraped the saucers that his pie came on. When Noah laughed at him, Cy winked.

"Can't let such wonderful food go to waste, now can I?"

"More likely it will go to your waist."

Cy drew himself up as he patted his flat stomach.

"No worries there, my friend. I know how to stay in shape."

"Well, it sure isn't with your diet. If you keep eating like that, your shape will be round."

"Ha ha! You're hilarious, you know it?"

At that point, they noticed an attractive older couple approaching their table. The woman gave Cy and Noah a wide smile as she introduced herself and her husband.

"Hi, I'm Christy Michaels and this is my husband, David. Are you new to our town? I don't remember seeing you here before."

Both men came to their feet and shook hands.

"I'm Noah Jameson and this is my friend Cy Wilkerson. Yes, we're new to town. We're here for, uh, personal business."

Christy beamed at them.

"Well, welcome to Forrestville. Listen, David and I are having a barbecue at our property outside of town on Sunday night. It's for our Sunday School class, but we also invite friends and family so you are welcome to join us."

Noah opened his mouth to decline, but before he could get the words out, Cy jumped in.

"That sounds great! What time should we be there? Do you want us to bring anything?"

"Come at 6:00. Our property is easy to find. Just go east down Highway 80 about five miles and look for a large brick mailbox on the right. Don't worry about bringing anything since we usually have more food than gets eaten."

Noah shot his friend an amused glance.

"It will get eaten this time," he chuckled. "You can count on that."

"That's everything I have at this point, Mr. Sinclair. Of course, if you need anything else, you can reach me on my cell phone. I really appreciate your letting me work on this project virtually."

"Not a problem, Noah. The work you're doing on the Stanley account doesn't require your presence in the office, so telework is appropriate. Is everything going all right?"

Noah thought about his encounter with Maggie the day before, and the events that followed. It seemed he was just biding his time, waiting to be allowed to get to know his son.

His son! The words filled him with wonder.

"Noah? Are you still there? Is everything okay?"

"Yes, sir. Sorry about that. I'm afraid my mind wandered for a moment. Everything is fine, and the project is coming along well, so I should have the final numbers to you by next Wednesday."

"Excellent. Well, call if you need anything."

Noah hung up and turned to take in the room he had rented at the bed and breakfast. The homey room boasted a large four-poster bed and private bathroom. It also included a coffee maker and small refrigerator. But, after staring at numbers all morning, Noah felt the need to go outside for some fresh air and to stretch his legs. A long walk around town to explore the small town where his ex-wife served as police chief seemed like an excellent idea.

After he closed his laptop and grabbed his keys and wallet, Noah found his way to the front door of the inn and out into the street. He strolled down the well-kept sidewalk with his hands in his pockets, admiring the occasional chalk picture at his feet.

Noah spotted the sign for the martial arts school and remembered that Robert had told him he was studying for his junior black belt in karate. He experienced a sudden desire to check out the school - wait, what was it called? A dojo! Yeah, he would peek inside the dojo and try to spot Robert. Noah would like to watch his son learning self-defense. If he was half as good as Maggie, the kid would be formidable.

Children and adults crowded along the sides of the small gymnasium as various students demonstrated moves from the different martial arts disciplines. A young boy in white, wearing a brown belt, stood holding a long stick. Noah heard someone in the crowd call it a "bo." His heart gave an extra thump when he recognized the boy as Robert.

His son manipulated the bo through a series of moves, which left Noah in awe. He couldn't help thinking he would not want to be on the receiving end of that thing in Robert's hands.

Noah stayed in the back throughout the class, observing as parents collected their children and left, the young students turning to bow to their instructors. During his time there, he had learned two more words. The students called the instructors "senseis" and they wore "gis." Now he knew four martial arts words, he thought. Maybe he would understand a little more when Robert discussed his class.

"Can I help you, sir?"

Noah turned to see a petite young woman in a white gi with a black belt loosely knotted around her rounded abdomen. When he noticed the wary expression on her face, he realized how suspicious he must seem. Noah scrambled for an explanation.

"I, uh, I've never been in a dojo before."

The young woman arched an eyebrow, as if waiting for a better reason for his presence.

Noah sighed.

"I met one of your students yesterday and when I saw your school, I mean dojo, I wanted to watch him. He said he was studying for his black belt test soon."

"Oh! You mean Robert!"

The boy heard his name and turned to wave at them. He trotted off the mat, his face beaming.

"Hi Mr. Jameson! Did you see my kata?"

Noah couldn't help the confused expression that crossed his face. The boy laughed as he explained the word.

"A kata is a series of moves in martial arts."

Noah had to chuckle at his ignorance.

"Wow! Now I've learned five martial arts words. I just might understand a little about martial arts now."

He reached to ruffle Robert's hair, but stopped himself from the affectionate gesture and reached to scratch his own head instead. Noah lowered his hand and grinned at his son.

"Yeah, I saw you. You looked pretty scary with that, what's it called? Bo?"

Robert returned the grin before turning to the young woman.

"Mr. Jameson, this is my martial arts instructor, Sensei Esther Abrams. Sensei, this is my mother's friend, Mr. Jameson. He's just visiting in town."

Esther offered her hand to shake, the skepticism on her face softening to a cautious greeting.

"Welcome to Forrestville, Mr. Jameson. How long are you planning to stay?"

Noah shrugged as he shook her hand.

"I'm not sure yet. I have some personal business to attend to that has an indefinite time for it."

Noah almost cringed at the vague answer that even sounded suspicious to him. As he tried to think of a way to clarify without explaining the whole story, movement across the room caught his attention. He spotted a large black German Shepherd that rose from a well-used cushion and trotted toward them. The dog reminded him of the narcotics dogs that passed through the jails and court-rooms he had sat in during his drug-using days.

He looked from the dog to Esther and wondered if she was one of Maggie's officers. Although he knew he had done nothing wrong, Noah's nerves thrummed with tension. He tried to turn his attention back to the conversation between instructor and student.

Maggie breathed in the crisp fall air as she hurried to the dojo. She had wanted to get there while Robert's class was in session so she could watch him show his kata, but another phone call from Emma had kept her. Now she was walking so quickly she was almost running. Maggie had to force herself to slow down.

As she stepped into the school, Maggie spotted Noah talking with Esther and Robert. She skidded to a halt just inside the door, anger welling up inside her. What was he doing here? She almost ran over to confront him, but stopped when Esther's German Shepherd got up and moved to join the trio.

Aha! Ninja was a former narcotics K9 officer. If Noah was doing drugs, he might still have the odor on him. Ninja would alert, then Maggie could ...

What? What could she do? She couldn't arrest him unless he had the drugs on him. But, if Ninja alerted, she would order Noah to stay away from her and Robert. Perhaps she would even threaten legal action.

Maggie stepped behind a rack of martial arts t-shirts and observed, her heart doing double time from the walk and the shock of seeing Noah near Robert. She noticed how age and maturity had made Noah more attractive. There seemed to be a steadiness about him that had been missing in their early years together.

She also noticed that Esther was looking between Robert and Noah, her expression puzzled. Maggie understood when Esther recognized the resemblance between the two. Seeing them together, it was hard to miss. Though Robert had Maggie's blue eyes, his thick, dark hair and dimples were just like Noah's. She almost groaned in aggravation at the realization that her friends would want an explanation that Maggie wasn't sure she wanted to give.

Before she could continue with that thought, Ninja stood next to Noah and reached his sensitive nose upward. Maggie waited for the big dog to sit next to Noah, the signal that he scented drugs on him. Instead, the shepherd nudged his massive head under Noah's hand, showing that he wanted to be petted. Maggie stood in disbelief as Noah reached down with a grin and scratched the dog behind his ears.

Maggie's brain buzzed with confusion as she eased out of the dojo. She knew she had witnessed Noah and Cy standing outside the town bar the day before. Both were known drug users and Cy had been arrested multiple times for dealing.

It occurred to Maggie that just because the K9 had not detected drugs on Noah did not mean he was not drinking. She would not let him near Robert until she was satisfied that he was neither drinking nor using. That meant she would have to keep a close eye on Noah.

Maggie would not let him hurt Robert like he had hurt her.

Chapter 6

Maggie settled into the pew and laid her Bible next to her. Since Forrestville was a quiet town most of the time, she did not have to keep a full crew at the station on Sundays. She usually kept three officers there on a rotating basis, including herself in that rotation. Maggie was glad this was one of her Sundays off. With the events of the past few days, she felt the need for the peace she often found in corporate prayer and worship.

Robert sat a few pews ahead of her, his head bent next to his friend's. That morning he had begged to sit with his friend, instead of with his mother. The two boys whispered and laughed. Maggie didn't intervene yet, but she would if they didn't stop when the service began.

Maggie experienced a pang of sadness as she watched her son. He was growing up so fast! She hoped to maintain the closeness they enjoyed. Soon he would have other interests, maybe a girlfriend. Maggie thought he would grow into a handsome man, like his father, Noah. Her ex-husband's moss green eyes and engaging smile filled her thoughts.

No! She would not allow her mind to go there. She jerked her attention back to the service, picking up a hymnal when the music director invited them all to stand and sing. Maggie found the song in the hymnal and opened her mouth to sing.

"May I join you?"

Maggie looked up into those same green eyes she wanted to put out of her mind. Noah seemed uncertain of his welcome. Resentment spurted in her heart at the way he put her on the spot by asking to sit with her. If she said no, she would seem cold and un-Christlike. But she so did not want this man anywhere near her!

Without a word, Maggie moved over to allow Noah to stand beside her. She handed him the hymnal, showed him which song, and picked up another song book.

"Thank you."

The swelling voices around them almost drowned out his words. Maggie just nodded and sang along, her alto voice soon rising to join the chorus. Noah stood in silence for a moment, then joined in the singing. Maggie had forgotten about his pleasant baritone voice. She remembered how often she had teased him about becoming a professional singer.

When the song ended, the pastor encouraged the congregation to turn to greet each other. All over the sanctuary, people shook hands or hugged. Maggie turned to the woman on the other side of her to speak a few words of greeting. When she turned around, David and Christy Michaels were standing in the aisle, greeting Noah.

"We're so glad you joined us today, Noah! Good morning, Maggie!"

Maggie saw a speculative gleam in Christy's eyes and wished she had stayed home. Then she wouldn't have seen Noah and the Michaels would not have witnessed them sitting together. Her friend was a sweet, good-hearted woman who loved to see everyone happy. Christy had been trying to match-make for Maggie almost since they first met.

"You two are still planning to come to our barbecue, aren't you? We don't have a service tonight. This is our night for fellowship, which means lots of food!"

David and Christy laughed, and Noah joined in. Maggie managed a half-hearted chuckle.

"Yes, Robert and I plan to be there."

When she saw the puzzled expressions on her friends' faces at her pointed exclusion of Noah, Maggie felt a little ashamed. But she would not change her words or allow herself to be paired with this man!

"Cy and I will be there. Thank you again for the invitation."

Wait! The Michaels invited Noah and Cyrus Wilkinson? Maggie considered backing out, then decided against it. No reason she and Robert needed to give up an evening with friends. She would just stay as far as possible from those two men. She hoped she could keep Robert away from them, too. It would be difficult to prevent her friendly, outgoing son from befriending the two men.

After the Michaels moved on to their seats, Maggie moved several spaces down from Noah during the rest of the song service. By the time the preaching started, she was sitting in the middle of the pew with Noah sitting near the aisle. Well, at least he showed the sense not to move closer to her.

Even sitting several feet from him, his spicy aftershave emitted an aroma that followed her. She remembered how much she had loved that scent during their marriage, even taking one of his t-shirts to sleep with when they were apart. She tried to steel herself against the fragrance and the memories, but they wouldn't leave her alone.

The pastor preached about forgiveness, but Maggie tuned him out. Her thoughts distracted her with rage that Noah Jameson dared to show up in her life again and ask to be a part of Robert's life. He didn't want to be a part of their child's life when she got pregnant or when she told Noah she wanted him to stay away from her and the child. It sure would not happen now, especially after she saw him standing in front of Pot O' Gold with a known drug dealer.

It just would not happen!

Noah stood by the bonfire at the Michaels' home and looked around with interest. He appreciated the natural beauty of the property and how the house blended with the forest instead of standing out. He glimpsed the large pond and wondered if the Michaels stocked it for fishing.

"Hello you two! I'm so glad you made it!"

Christy approached the small group around the bonfire and shook Noah's hand. She smiled at Cy, who juggled a hot dog in one hand and a cup of cider in the other. The big man gave her a sheepish grin.

"Sorry I can't shake your hand, ma'am, but I'm enjoying the delicious food you've prepared."

Christy laughed and waved her hand toward the food tables.

"That's what it's here for," she assured him. "Dig in."

Noah put his hand on his chest as he pretended to tremble with fear.

"Oh, no! You shouldn't have told him that. Now there won't be any for the rest of us."

Cy scowled at him.

"Don't give her the wrong idea, Noah. I'm not that greedy. Just a growing boy."

"Yeah, and growing, and growing."

As the group laughed and joked, Noah watched a small SUV pull up and park. When he saw the blond woman and dark-haired boy get out of the vehicle, his heartbeat tripled. He had forgotten that Maggie and Robert would be here. He wondered how it was possible for him to have forgotten an important detail like that.

Christy followed his gaze, and her smile widened. She turned to welcome the newcomers.

"Maggie! I'm so glad you're here. Let me introduce you to a couple of new friends, Cyrus Wilkinson and Noah Jameson. Oh, well, you were sitting with Noah in church this morning, weren't you? Anyway, Cy and Noah, this our police chief, Maggie Jones, and her son, Robert."

Although the late October evening was warm, to Noah the temperature dropped about twenty degrees when Maggie's eyes landed on him. Her body language was stiff and unwelcoming.

"We did not attend church together."

Both Christy and Robert looked askance at Maggie for the icy tone she used. Noah guessed she was not normally so chilly toward newcomers. He thought they had made a little progress at her office the day he arrived, so this hostility surprised him.

"Uh, Maggie, can you come with me, please? I need your help up at the house for a minute."

Christy pulled on Maggie's arm to move her away from the small group.

"I'd rather not leave Robert here, alone with these strangers."

Noah stiffened. Why was she treating him like an enemy?

"It will be all right. David will keep an eye on him."

While Christy still tugged on her reluctant guest, Robert looked from his mother to Noah, his expression puzzled at his mother's odd behavior. His blue eyes swept the small group, then came back to rest on his mother's face. Though he still seemed concerned about the way his mother was acting, he gave her a wave and a grin.

"Mom, I'll be fine. Go ahead with Ms. Christy."

With that, the boy picked up a skewer and threaded a wiener on it. His mother watched him for a moment, her lips in a thin line. Finally, she let her curious hostess lead her into the house.

"Okay, Maggie, that was very unusual behavior for you. I've never heard you use that tone of voice with someone unless it was a suspect. What's up?"

Maggie turned to the kitchen counter, looking for something to do with her hands while she fought the tears that pricked the back of her eyes. She found a sponge and wiped the already clean surface with hands that trembled.

When Christy's arms came around her, Maggie stiffened before relaxing into her friend's comforting hug. Christy led her away from the kitchen, into a small study lined with bookcases. She pointed Maggie to a comfortable rocker and seated herself in a nearby recliner.

"Sweetie, what's wrong?"

Maggie gulped in a deep breath. She had hoped to keep her past in the past, but with Noah's reappearance in her life, she realized she would have to tell her story. She believed Christy to be a sweet, caring lady who would keep her confidence.

"I'm not ready for this to be common knowledge," she hedged.

Christy nodded her understanding.

"Noah Jameson is my ex-husband."

Christy sat back in surprise. She looked out the window, where they could view the group by the bonfire. She tapped her chin, then looked back at Maggie.

"I thought there was something familiar about Noah. Robert favors him. But, why the hostility? Was it a bad break-up?"

Maggie had thought to only tell the bare minimum about their divorce, but found it all pouring out to Christy's sympathetic ears. She told about their early years when they were so in love, his downward spiral into drugs and alcohol, and his callous reaction when she told him she was pregnant. Tears flowed freely as she unburdened herself.

Christy handed her a box of tissues.

"The last time I saw him is seared in my mind. I don't think I'll ever forget it."

The squad cars approached the property with no lights or sirens. They parked and police officers spilled out onto the street and driveway. The house was lit from top to bottom, and sounds of music and raucous laughter filtered out.

Maggie and Monica stood waiting for instructions from the police officer in charge of the raid. They had received a tip that there was a party in this house and that drugs were present.

Monica looked at Maggie with a question in her eyes. Maggie glanced at her commander, then back at her friend. She shook her head a little.

"You know you have to tell them soon." Monica whispered.

"I know, but not yet," Maggie whispered back with a cautious glance around them.

"I don't want to be put on desk duty yet."

"*Maggie!*"

Maggie sighed and gave her friend's shoulder a light bump with her fist.

"*I'll tell them tomorrow, okay? And I'll be careful tonight. Do you think I would do anything to put the baby at risk? But I just feel like I need to be here tonight. I don't know why, but the feeling is really strong.*"

"*Well, I don't like it, but okay. I'm keeping my eye on you though.*"

"*I'd rather you keep an eye out for trouble-and stay out of it!*"

Maggie and Monica turned their attention to the whispered instructions and hand motions of their commander. They approached the house and looked at the officer at the door.

In a flash, the police were in the house commanding the occupants to freeze and raise their hands. Those who resisted faced pistols held by determined officers. Bottles of whiskey and vodka sat on tables next to straight lines of white powder that waited to be inhaled.

Maggie and Monica joined other officers who swept the rooms, looking for more party-goers and drugs. They entered a room with several people in various stages of intoxication. Maggie's stomach roiled at the sights and smells. Then she saw him.

The man draped across the end of the bed, a half-full bottle of whiskey in his hand. His pockets were full of small bags of white powder. His greasy hair hung limply in his bloodshot eyes. Noah looked up at her, his eyes widening in surprise. He sat up and ran his hand through his hair with a feral snarl on his face.

Monica stepped up beside her and tapped her on the shoulder. When Maggie turned to see her friend, the understanding and sympathy in Monica's eyes almost undid her self-control.

"Mags, I think they need your help in the living room so I'll take care of this one."

Maggie nodded her thanks, before turning to take in the drunk weaving in front of her. This was not the same man she had fallen in love with! As Monica snapped the handcuffs on him, Maggie gave him one last look of pain and disgust, then turned and walked out of the room.

"And that was the last time you saw him until day before yesterday?"

"Yes. I let my lawyer handle the divorce because I wanted nothing from Noah except for him to stay away. He seemed happy to comply."

"What's he doing here now?"

Maggie felt the anger rising inside her as she remembered seeing Noah in front of the town's only bar with a known felon.

"He says he's gotten right with God and wants to make amends. He also claims he got off the drugs and alcohol. But I caught him standing in front of Pot O' Gold not 30 minutes after we talked in my office; and that man with him is someone I remember arresting for drug dealing when I worked with the Shreveport police."

A horrified expression crossed Christy's face.

"Oh, Maggie! I'm so sorry! That shows I need to be more careful who I invite out here. I just saw two newcomers and wanted to be welcoming."

Maggie patted Christy's hand.

"I know, Christy. You have such a warm heart that sees the best in everybody. Don't worry about it, though. I'm watching them while they're in town."

She cast another baleful look at the two men, who were laughing and talking with David.

"Just let them step out of line. I'll be right on them."

Christy followed her gaze.

"Are you sure he's still on drugs or alcohol? I didn't smell anything on them when we met them at the diner, but I did witness both men bowing their heads to bless their food. Is it possible they have changed?"

Maggie shook her head, her expression skeptical.

"I don't know Christy. Maybe. Or it's possible they put on a show to give a false impression. I guess time will tell, but I will keep a close eye on them. Especially Noah. He wants to be a part of Robert's life, but I can't allow that. My son doesn't know Noah is his father. I told him his father was dead because I didn't want Noah's drug and alcohol habit to touch him. Now all I want is to make sure my ex-husband doesn't hurt Robert."

Christy gave her a wise look.

"Is it Robert that you don't want hurt? Or yourself?"

Maggie followed Christy back out to the bonfire near the pond. As they got closer to Noah, Maggie felt herself stiffening again. Seeing Noah standing in front of the town's bar had brought back a lot of painful memories that she believed she had buried. She realized that what she'd really like to do was pitch her ex-husband into the nearby pond. A grim smile crossed her face at the idea. She cleared her expression when she arrived at the tables where her son ate and laughed with the surrounding group.

Robert gave his mother a guilty look when her eyes rested on his plate, which he had piled high with two hot dogs and a mound of chips. She shook her head at the sight.

As a rule, Maggie tried to keep Robert from overindulging on junk food, but since tonight was a special night visiting with friends, she just smiled at him.

"Go ahead, son, but don't overdo. I don't want to be up all night listening to you be sick."

"I won't get sick, Mom."

Christy handed Maggie a plate and motioned toward the food, but Maggie's appetite had disappeared. She set the plate down and stepped to Noah's side.

"May I have a word with you?"

She tried to make her voice neutral, but it still came out icy and hard.

Noah set down his plate and followed Maggie to a quieter area away from the bonfire. He wondered again why she acted so hostile toward him and what she wanted now. Would she demand he leave town? His ex-wife answered those questions when she stopped and fixed him with a glare.

"I saw you after you left my office."

Noah hesitated as he remembered where he had gone that day. His heart sank when he realized she must have seen him at Pot O' Gold. But didn't she see him leave without entering the bar?

"I will not have you coming around my son drunk or on drugs!"

That answered his question.

"Maggie."

He reached to touch her arm, but reconsidered that move when he recognized the thunderous expression on her face. He stepped back and turned to face the pond, his jaw clenched. After a moment he spoke, his voice soft at first, then gaining in strength and volume.

"I won't lie to you. After our discussion, I wanted a drink. But I've come so far and don't want to go back, so I asked God for help, and you know what?"

Noah turned back to Maggie, his face shining in the moonlight.

"He took away my desire for alcohol! Then he sent Cy to provide encouragement and support. In fact, Cy prayed for me right there in front of the bar. Then we left and went to MaryAnn's for lunch. I did not touch any alcohol, Maggie, and I still have had no alcohol or drugs for over five years."

Maggie shot him a skeptical look.

"After all the grief you gave me about trusting in God and going to church, you expect me to believe you prayed?"

Resentment surged inside Noah. He was doing his best to show her he had changed, but she wouldn't even meet him half-way. He thought about Robert and struggled to control the anger. For his son's sake, he would continue his efforts to get Maggie to understand.

"Maggie, don't you believe God changes people?"

When her expression turned stormy, Noah hastened to add.

"I'm not trying to use God or faith to manipulate you. I only want you to consider that He could change me. He did change me! Please, give me a chance to show you I am not the drug addict and drunkard that hurt you in the past. Because of God's grace and mercy I am a different man now."

Noah met his ex-wife's incredulous eyes with an open and honest gaze. After a moment, she turned away and stood watching the bonfire. Her shoulders slumped a fraction of an inch, and she didn't look at him as she spoke.

"I'll give you another chance."

Here she turned and gave him a fierce scowl.

"But if I smell even a whiff of alcohol on you or see any hint of drug use, you will get nowhere near my son. Is that understood?"

Our son, Noah thought. He kept that quiet for now.

"I understand."

Chapter 7

Maggie turned over and adjusted her pillow again. She wasn't sure why, but she felt restless, as if she needed to do something but didn't know what. Maggie flopped over onto her back and laid her arm on her head as she released a deep sigh.

She understood what the problem was - Noah reappearing in her life. Maggie could see that there had been some appreciable changes in him, but letting go of the past proved to be difficult. When they married, they had been so much in love, but the drugs and the alcohol took him away from her. The day she told him she didn't want to see him again, it had hurt so badly Maggie still couldn't believe she got the words out of her mouth. Staying away before and after the divorce took every ounce of willpower in her soul.

Maggie sat up and reached for her slippers, thinking a cup of hot chamomile tea might help soothe her nerves. When she reached the door of her bedroom, a muffled noise came to her ears. Maggie paused, holding her breath. There! That was not a normal sound in her house, especially at night. She slipped back to her nightstand and picked up her pistol. Maggie eased the door open and slid into the hallway, then paused in front of Robert's partially open door. She scanned his room until satisfied the noise had not come from there. Once assured of his safety, she closed his door and continued down the hall.

As Maggie moved toward the front of the house, she heard Bear growling. Surprised, she picked up her pace. The Rottweiler seldom growled, snarled, or barked.

She entered the living room in time to hear a man's voice yell something about a bear. A dark figure in a black ski mask leaned halfway through a side window. The intruder tried to pull back as Bear lunged toward him, snarling and barking. The man struck his elbow on the window and something fell out of his hand onto the living room floor. His head barely cleared the window frame before the big dog snapped at the place his arm just left.

"Stop! Police!"

Maggie aimed her gun at the window, but with Bear standing in the way, she hesitated to fire. Instead, she ran to the window and watched as the intruder ran through the backyard, heading for the gate leading to the woods. Maggie called the Rottweiler to her, then opened the back door.

"Get him!"

Bear needed no further encouragement. He bounded out the door and raced for the figure that stood fumbling with desperate fingers to open the back gate. When the intruder couldn't get the catch to open, he scrambled over. The Rottweiler snapped at his heels as he got to the top of the gate, then jumped into the low bushes behind the yard and disappeared into the dark forest behind the yard.

The dog stood watching, growls still rumbling from his throat. Maggie hated not catching the intruder, but scratched the dog on the head when he trotted back to her.

"Good boy, Bear. You ran him off."

She gazed into the woods that now seemed dark and threatening to her.

"Still, I wish we could have caught him."

Bear's expression said he wished he had caught him, too.

When they reentered the house, the big dog headed for the window where the intruder tried to enter and sniffed at an object laying near the wall. Maggie turned on the light to inspect the item.

"What did you find, boy?"

She bent over to see what Bear found, then stepped into the kitchen and grabbed a plastic sandwich bag. When Maggie returned to the living room, she picked up the object, using the sandwich bag to preserve any fingerprints, and held it in her hand.

It was a black hunting knife, with the initials MS carved into the handle. Although well made, the knife emanated a sinister presence. Maggie sealed it in the plastic bag and slid her cell phone out of her pocket to call the station.

"Send a couple of officers to my house. Someone tried to break in tonight."

Maggie didn't need to give her address, but she checked to make sure the outside light was on so her house would be easy to find. Then she went to her room and changed into jeans and a sweater. She wouldn't be getting any sleep that night, so after changing, she headed toward the kitchen to make a pot of coffee.

"Mom? What's going on?"

Maggie whirled to see her son plodding down the hall toward the living room, his hair sticking in every direction and his eyes bleary with sleep. Bear trotted to his side and sidled in to get a head scratch.

"Someone tried to break in."

"Wow! Really? Did you shoot him? Did Bear get him?"

Even though she was still shaking with fear and outrage at the thought of the intruder in her home, Maggie had to smile at his enthusiasm. To her, it seemed the intruder had violated her sanctuary, but to Robert, the break-in was an exciting adventure. With a jolt, she remembered the knife dropped on the floor and stopped smiling. If that man succeeded in getting inside, what did he intend to do with that knife?

Maggie stared at Bear, her thoughts whirling. If not for the big dog's presence in the living room, the intruder would have gotten inside and this night could have had a much more deadly ending. Maggie crossed the room to drape her arm across her son's shoulders.

"You know what, Robert?"

The boy stopped rubbing on the dog's head at the serious tone in his mother's voice.

"What?"

"Bear protected our house tonight and chased the intruder away, so I think he has earned a forever home with us. "

Robert cheered as Maggie knelt next to the Rottweiler and encircled his thick neck with her arms. She held back the tears as their new family member gave her cheek a sloppy kiss. With a big squeeze and a kiss on his furry head, Maggie expressed her gratitude to their canine hero.

"Thank you, Bear. Welcome home."

Zach jerked awake at the sound of the cabin door slamming open. He struggled to sit up in his sleeping bag and rubbed his eyes as his friend stomped into the cabin. Mickey seemed riled about something and when he got riled, things got ugly. Zach shrank into his sleeping bag and wished he could hide until Mickey's foul mood cleared. He lay still, watching Mickey stomp around the small space, then got up with a sigh to turn on the battery-powered lantern and fix a pot of coffee on the small propane stove.

After listening to Mickey mutter curses about "that witch" and "ruined my life," Zach worked up the nerve to ask him what happened.

"What happened?! That... that stupid woman almost shot me! She has a gigantic dog in her house that nearly took my arm off when I tried to get in the house. She sicced him on me and he almost got my leg. If I hadn't been too smart and fast for her and that monster, they would have killed me!"

Zach took the pot off the stove and poured the thick, black brew into tin cups. He handed one to Mickey, who accepted it with a grunt and took a large gulp.

Although he was almost afraid to ask, Zach's curiosity overwhelmed his fear.

"Why, I mean, what were you doing at her house?"

Mickey took another long slurp of his coffee before looking up with an evil grin.

"I planned to cut her throat while she slept."

Mickey jerked, almost spilling his coffee. With frantic motions, he reached for the sheath on his belt. When he found it empty, he started cursing again.

"What's wrong, Mick?"

"My knife! I must have dropped it when that dog sc... startled me. That's my favorite knife, too! Just another time that woman has ruined my life."

Zach had heard Mickey complain so many times about Maggie Jones ruining his life, he had to ask.

"Hey, Mickey, how did she ruin your life?"

Mickey stopped and stared at Zach for so long the younger man squirmed.

"I done told you, didn't I?"

Mickey had never told him the entire story, but Zach knew better than to correct him. He gave him an apologetic shrug and fibbed.

"I forgot. Please tell me again. I really want to know."

Mickey nodded, as if pleased by his younger friend's eagerness for the story.

"I had a sweet deal going about ten, eleven years ago. Had a pretty wife, a son, and a solid business selling cocaine in Shreveport to my special 'clientele.' I tell you, I was making some good money. Had my own house and a nice car. Then that witch arrested me on a drug rap and when I went to trial, Maggie Jones even turned my wife against me. Got her to testify in court that I beat her. I never beat my wife! I might have slapped her around a time or two when she sassed me, but I didn't beat her."

Zach had never met the woman, but he could imagine his friend abusing her. He wondered again why he continued to hang around with Mickey, but turned his attention back to the story.

"After that, everything went downhill. I served time, well, you know. That's where we met and got to be such good friends."

Zach barely kept from shrinking away from Mickey's evil leer. He often doubted Mickey was that good of a friend.

"When I got out, my suppliers treated me like dirt. Said I wasn't 'reliable' enough to sell for them. My woman left me while I was in prison. She took the boy and disappeared, so I never found them. It's all Maggie Jones' fault and I'm going to kill her for it!"

"What about your knife? Can they trace you with that?"

Mickey shook his head in disgust.

"You can be so stupid sometimes, you know it? No, they can't trace me, 'cause I had gloves on. It has initials, but they could belong to anyone. I can get another knife, but that one was my favorite."

He stood with a grunt and lumbered to a metal box with a secured padlock. After twisting the dial a few times, Mickey popped open the lock and reached inside, removing a large pistol and a cleaning kit. He returned to his seat and began the methodical task of disassembling and cleaning the gun. As he worked, Mickey's face took on a thoughtful expression.

After he finished cleaning the gun and returned the kit to the box, Mickey loaded the weapon and sat holding it and looking around the small cabin. He lifted the gun and aimed it at a dusty clay pitcher perched on top of an empty crate. Zach bit his tongue to keep from begging him to not fire the gun in the cabin. He knew it would only goad Mickey to do it just to show he could.

After a moment, a shot echoed in the enclosed space, causing Zach's ears to ring. The clay pitcher lay shattered on the floor and Mickey peered around the room in search of another target. His mouth stretched into a malevolent sneer as he pointed the pistol at Zach. The younger man stumbled back with his hands in front of him.

"Mickey! What are you doing? You're not going to shoot me! I'm your friend!"

Mickey continued to aim the barrel at Zach as he laughed at his expression. Finally, he lowered the gun and Zach dared to take a breath. Mickey snorted as he laid the gun on the table.

"You are such an idiot! Did you really think I would shoot you?"

He got up and moved to stand in front of Zach, putting a meaty paw on his friend's shoulder as he continued to chuckle at Zach's discomfort.

"Don't worry, Zach. I wouldn't hurt you. Like you said, you're my friend."

The big man guffawed.

"Anyway, you're still of some use to me."

Zach released a nervous laugh.

"Yeah, you had me going there for a minute."

He thought for a minute before asking the question that burned in his thoughts.

"Mick, are you planning to shoot the police chief?"

Mickey considered the idea for a moment, then shook his head.

"Nah, too much noise and too many ways it can go wrong."

The smile on his ugly face sent a ripple of revulsion through Zach.

"I prefer the personal touch a knife provides."

He checked the door, then struggled into his sleeping bag. Zach turned off the lantern and got into his own bed. As he drifted off to sleep, Mickey's voice came to him in the darkness.

"I'll get another chance, though. You watch. Maggie Jones will die!"

Zach sniffed and wiped his nose with the back of his hand, then added a couple of sticks to the fire in front of him. Even with the warmth coming from the blaze, he still felt cold and miserable. He wished Mickey had not insisted that Zach come with him to this beat-up old shack in the woods near Forrestville.

Resentment surged through Zach. When they arrived, he'd gotten a glimpse of the pretty sidewalks and attractive storefronts and wanted to take a walk to get a closer look. But Mickey just swore at him and told him they weren't there for sightseeing. Since settling in the shack, Mickey did all the foraging for food or running errands in town. Zach stayed out of sight at the cabin .

He sighed. Maybe everyone was right. He was a loser whose only friend was a crazy guy who plotted to hurt the cop who arrested him. Zach heard the voices again.

Boy, you'll never amount to anything. You're useless, just like your daddy.

That was what his mother always told him. His father left when Zach was a baby. He showed up whenever he pleased to play a game of catch or tell a couple of stories. Then he would mooch some money from his wife and disappear again.

There were other voices, too.

You're such a loser.

You can't do anything right.

You're so stupid.

Mickey called him names too, but at least he stuck around. Zach didn't have anyone else. His mother died, and he had no siblings. Mickey was about the only "family" Zach had.

A rustle to his right caused Zach to start back and drop the stick he was using to poke the fire. When a large black and brown dog came bounding through the brush, Zach's heart seized, thinking it was a bear. When he recognized the animal was a Rottweiler, fear gripped him even more strongly. His mind filled with images of savage fighting dogs ripping into flesh; *his* flesh. He sat frozen, unable to move.

"Here, boy! Come!"

A young boy's voice sounded behind the dog. A moment later, Zach saw the boy following the dog into the clearing. The youngster stopped at the sight of Zach while the dog sniffed around the campfire where Zach was roasting wieners.

"Sorry, mister, I didn't know you were here. Bear! Heel!"

With one hungry sniff, the dog made his way to the boy's side and sat panting.

Zach relaxed and allowed a small smile. He had a soft spot for kids and he realized now that the dog wouldn't hurt him.

"That's okay, kid. You're not bothering me. What's your dog's name?"

"Bear. We call him that because he looks like a bear."

"Yeah, he does. That's a good name for him."

Zach noticed the boy eying the hot dogs.

"Would you like to roast a hot dog with me? You can even give your dog one."

The boy hesitated, and Zach realized someone probably taught him not to accept food from strangers.

"My name is Zach. What's yours?"

He slid the package of hot dogs and a couple of whittled sticks toward the kid.

"I'm Robert. Why are you out here in the woods? Are you camping?"

Zach had a story ready for anyone who came upon him.

"Yeah, my friend and me like cold weather camping. It's less crowded."

Robert considered that for a moment, then nodded.

"Yeah, I guess I can get that."

He stepped up to the fire and selected a stick and a hot dog. Threading the point of the stick deep into the wiener, he plopped himself onto a nearby stump and held the meat over the fire.

"Thanks for the hot dog, Zach! I was kind of hungry after exploring the woods. Are you sure it's okay for me to give my dog one?"

Zach assented and watched as the dog ate his treat in two bites. He listened as Robert talked all about his adventures in the woods that morning. It was nice to have company, but he guessed he better send the boy away before Mickey got back. Mickey didn't like kids or dogs, especially since he said a dog nearly killed him when he broke into the police chief's house. Of course, Mickey looked nothing like a dog did anything to him, but Zach wouldn't contradict him.

He brought his attention back to Robert, who had stopped talking and was looking at him with a quizzical expression.

"Are you okay, Zach? You had a funny look on your face just now."

Zach tried to laugh it off.

"Oh, I'm fine. Just remembered something I need to do. I'll have to send you on your way, now, kid. My break time is over and I gotta get back to work."

Before Robert could ask him what kind of work he needed to do in the middle of the woods, Zach stood up and brushed himself off, as if he had lots to do.

"Thanks for stopping by. Hope I see you again."

Robert took the not-so-subtle hint and stood too, stuffing the rest of his hot dog in his mouth. He dusted off his hands and turned to Zach after swallowing the large bite. With a grin, he waved to his new friend and turned towards the path he arrived on.

"Thanks again for the hot dog. See you!"

Robert called his dog and tramped off into the woods. Zach heard the boy whistling as he went and smiled. Robert seemed like a good kid.

Chapter 8

Was this such a good idea?

Maggie hesitated in front of Kat's Nails. Christy had given her a gift certificate for her birthday and insisted that Maggie needed to pamper herself for a while. But Maggie felt her lifestyle was just not right for manicured nails.

She looked at her hands, taking in the callouses and short, unadorned nails. Maggie had always believed that keeping her nails clean and even was enough. Did she need polish and lotions and all that?

If she was honest with herself, Maggie thought, gossip was the real reason she didn't want to go in. She knew someone in town would have seen Noah sitting with her in church, and the rumor mill would churn away. Just thinking about listening to the women discussing her personal life made Maggie feel sick. She decided a manicure was not on her agenda for today.

Just as she turned away from the door, Maggie sensed someone watching her. She scanned the street, but couldn't see anything out of the ordinary.

"Maggie!"

Maggie almost groaned when she saw the owner of the nail salon approaching. Katie Smythe, also known as Kat, was a pretty young woman with shoulder-length blue hair which she adorned with glittering clips and headbands. Her long nails always looked like works of art. The shop owner's quirky sense of humor and sparkling personality made her a favorite in the small town.

Kat crossed the street toward the shop, her hands full with a tray of coffee cups and pastries. Now that the young woman had seen her, there was no way Maggie could get away.

"Hey, girl! I'm so glad you made it. Can you get the door for me? I don't want to drop our morning snack."

Maggie considered opening the door, then bolting, but she realized she couldn't do it. If she ran away it would upset Kat, and Maggie wouldn't hurt this sweet young lady for anything. So, she forced a smile and followed Kat into the shop.

Though small, the nail salon reflected Kat's artistic personality. She had everything set for comfort and practicality, even a small gift counter near the front. The blue and lavender color scheme provided a soothing ambiance, as did the soft instrumental music playing in the background. Maggie relaxed as she thought maybe this wouldn't be so bad.

Not that Maggie didn't like to be pampered or look pretty. She just felt she had too many other things to do, more important things. However, she knew her reluctance to come to the nail salon had more to do with the intimate atmosphere, which seemed to encourage gossip and sharing secrets. Maggie preferred to keep her private affairs to herself, and she didn't want to hear about the intimate details of other people's lives.

"Come on over here, Maggie, and let's get started. Can I get you something? A cup of coffee or tea? A bottle of water?"

Maggie accepted a cup of coffee, then took the comfortable chair in front of Kat. She perched on the edge, her muscles tense, as if ready to jump and run. Kat raised her eyebrows at her customer's rigid posture and gave her a gentle shove to encourage her to sit back.

"Relax, this is supposed to be fun."

The hand massage felt good, Maggie admitted to herself. And it was nice to have someone fuss over her a little. She settled more comfortably into the chair and allowed herself to enjoy the process.

Until the gossip started.

"Hey, Maggie, who was that hunk that came into the station last week?"

"Yeah, he's cute! I love that dimple."

"Didn't I see you sitting with him at church?"

"Wasn't he at the Michaels' Sunday night? You two were kind of cozy there for a few minutes, weren't you? Anything you want to share?"

The tension coiled in Maggie's stomach. Here we go, she thought. Gossip and secrets. She determined to keep the information to a minimum. There was no way she would tell anyone in this crowd about her marriage to Noah or the reason for their divorce. She replied in a clipped tone.

"He's someone I knew in Shreveport."

The ladies in the shop exchanged meaningful glances as they giggled. The eager expressions on their faces showed they knew she was holding out on them. Maggie sighed at the realization they wouldn't let her get away with anything less than the full story.

"What's he in town for?"

"Personal business."

"What kind of personal business?"

"Are you part of that business?"

That was enough. Maggie pulled her hands away from Kat's gentle massage and reached for her purse. She stood and took a step toward the door.

"I think I better go. You're getting way too personal for me. You know gossip is not my thing."

Maggie didn't want to be polite any more. Now she wanted out of this place.

Kat jumped to her feet and glared at the other women.

"You ladies leave her alone! She's here for pampering, not to satisfy your thirst for juicy details."

Another customer sitting nearby added her voice.

"Yeah, leave her alone! She doesn't have to answer your questions. Sheila, come back and finish my manicure. I got places to go when we're done here and I don't have time for a gossip fest."

"Oh, all right, Bebe, I'm coming!"

Sheila joined the woman sitting at her table, and the women murmured apologies as they returned to their seats. Bebe gave Maggie a supportive smile and winked at her. Kat reached out a detaining hand to her customer.

"Come on, Maggie, and sit back down. The ladies will leave you alone now, and you don't have to tell anybody anything you don't want to. Come on, please?"

Maggie stood and gazed around the shop. She gave serious consideration to leaving, but Kat's pleading expression changed her mind. The shop owner was a good friend, and she didn't want to hurt her feelings. She also didn't want to feed the rumor mill by storming out of the shop angry.

"Okay. But no gossip."

Kat nodded, her blue hair waving with the gesture as she reached for the tray of polishes.

"No gossip. Now, I think this rose pink is perfect for you. How do you like it?"

Maggie tried to relax as Kat painted her nails and chattered about mundane topics. She appreciated the young woman's attempt to put her at ease and even responded a few times.

The door to the shop opened with a harsh jangle of bells and an older man with a dirty, grizzled face poked his head inside. His dark eyes swept the room, stopping to stare at Maggie. For a moment his face emanated an intense malice, then he cleared his expression.

"Sorry to bother you," he muttered. "Just looking for someone." He pulled back, and the door closed with a thump as the room erupted in questions.

"Who was that?"

"Maggie, why did he glare at you like that? Do you know him?"

"No, I don't know him. Don't worry, ladies, I'll check him out. In the meantime, all of you be careful and make sure you are aware of your surroundings at all times."

Maggie didn't want to alarm the women in the shop, but the intruder seemed familiar. In fact, he reminded her of the man she had seen in the alley the previous week, right before the attack.

After a few more minutes of excited chatter, the women settled down and returned to their manicures and pedicures. The shop once again became a cozy space for pampering and quiet conversation. Kat pulled Maggie's hands out of the nail drier and held them where Maggie could see.

"There you go, my friend. All done."

The change in her hands was amazing. Kat had softened most of the callouses, and Maggie's nails were now a pretty oval shape that glistened with rosy polish.

"Kat, they look great! Thank you for taking such good care of me."

Maggie reached into her purse and pulled out her gift certificate and a ten-dollar bill, which she handed to Kat. The young woman accepted the certificate, but raised an eyebrow at the cash.

"What's this for?"

"That's your tip."

"No, ma'am. Today's trip was all about pampering you. It was a gift from Christy Michaels and she'd get very upset with both of us if I let you pay me anything."

"But, Kat, I want to show my appreciation for the magnificent job you did."

Kat gave her head an emphatic shake and handed the ten back with a smile. When Maggie tried again to give it to her, Kat put her hands behind her back.

"Are you *trying* to get me into trouble with Christy? No, ma'am. That manicure is her gift to you. Now, you have a wonderful day."

Maggie sighed.

"Okay, you win. I'm just going to check out your gift counter, then I need to go. Lots of things to do today."

The small gift counter held a nice selection of beauty merchandise. Maggie took her time as she browsed down its length. When another customer distracted Kat, Maggie took the ten-dollar bill and stuffed it in the tip jar on the counter. With a triumphant smile on her face, Maggie stepped out the door into the street. She swept the street with her gaze, searching for the strange man who disrupted her morning. When she didn't see him, Maggie took a step toward the book store. That was as far as she got before she heard a familiar voice behind her.

"Maggie!"

She turned to see Kat standing behind her, holding the ten.

"You forgot something."

"No, I don't think so."

Kat stood holding the ten-dollar bill out to her friend and Maggie had to admire Kat's tenacity.

"You really won't let me give you a tip?"

"Nope."

Maggie laughed and accepted the cash. Kat reached for her and gave her a big hug.

"Now, I mean it. Go have a wonderful day!"

After Kat returned to the salon, Maggie checked the street again. Though she no longer had the sense of being watched, the thought of the strange visitor to the shop and the expression of hate he directed at her gave Maggie an uneasy feeling.

What was this guy up to?

"Go get it, boy!"

Robert threw the disk as far as he could and grinned at the sight of Bear chasing it down the length of the park. He made a terrific choice in bringing his dog to play fetch at Forrestville Park. After all, he had the entire weekend in front of him and it was a great day to go out and have fun.

Bear trotted back to Robert, carrying the Frisbee, while his stump of tail wagged his entire back end. The boy laughed at the sight, his carefree voice carrying throughout the area. A few other park-goers looked up at the sound and smiled.

With sweat beading on his forehead, Robert plopped down onto a picnic bench and grabbed a bottle of water, tipping it up and draining the contents in one long gulp. Bear sat at his feet, watching every drop. He licked Robert's hand where a little of the water spilled.

The boy looked down, and with a sense of guilt, reached to scratch the dog behind the ears. Here he was guzzling water while his poor dog panted with thirst after playing fetch. Robert dug in his backpack and pulled out another water bottle and a small Styrofoam bowl, which he set on the ground. The Rottweiler nosed the bowl as if to hurry his friend along in pouring the water. Robert pushed his dog back a little and filled the bowl about half-way.

"There you go, Bear. Get a good drink so we can play some more."

The big dog lapped up every drop of the water, pushing the lightweight bowl around with his mouth.

Bear's head snapped up, and he gazed behind Robert. A thin young man in shabby clothes approached, his eyes riveted on the dog. Instead of growling or standing in front of Robert to protect him, Bear began whining and wagging his tail. He pranced up to the tramp and lay down in front of him.

"King? Is that you, boy? How're you doing?"

The man scratched Bear's head and neck and rubbed the big dog's belly when he rolled over. Robert watched his dog in amazement as Bear wiggled with joy. After staring at the stranger for a few minutes, Robert had to ask.

"Who are you, mister?"

The shabby young man stood from rubbing on the dog and dusted his hands off before offering one to Robert.

"My name is Kevin Willis. This is my dog."

Noah closed the spreadsheet and shut down his laptop. He sighed as he reached to knead the kinks out of his neck. His back complained from the long hours at the desk, so he stood to stretch, enjoying the soothing warmth on his shoulders from the sun streaming through the window.

I've been sitting and working at the computer for way too long, he thought. It's time to get out and walk a bit.

He remembered the park he had spied at the end of Main Street. A walk through the trees and around the small pond would be a perfect way to finish a long day of hard work. Noah stuffed his wallet in his back pocket and picked up his room key. He took a quick glance around the room before he exited. Noah couldn't help feeling like a schoolboy let out of class early.

As he approached the park, Noah noticed a young boy with dark brown hair throwing a Frisbee for a dog. His heart quickened when he recognized his son. Noah longed to insert himself into the game of fetch, but his heart sank when he remembered Maggie didn't want him around Robert when she was not present. He wanted the chance to get to know the boy, but realized he needed to tread carefully. If Maggie saw him alone with Robert, she might deny him any opportunity to have a part in his son's life.

Noah's eyes narrowed when he saw a shabby young man approach and lean over to pet on the Rottweiler. His reluctance to approach Robert disappeared in a surge of protectiveness and he quickened his pace until he stood near the trio. When the young man and the boy turned their attention to him, Noah stuck out his hand to introduce himself.

"Hi, I'm Noah. What's your name?"

Robert saw his mother's old friend, Mr. Jameson almost run up to him and Kevin and wondered why. A quick glance at Kevin's appearance reminded him he had suspected the shabby stranger at first, too. Bear's eager greeting provided the reassurance Robert needed that Kevin was okay.

After Kevin introduced himself to Noah, the two men stood watching each other in an awkward silence. Robert gave in to his curiosity and asked the questions that burned in his mind.

"Why did you leave Bear, uh, King at the grocery store? Why was he so thin? He looked like you didn't take care of him."

Too late, Robert realized he sounded like he was accusing Kevin, but he couldn't help it. He wanted to know why this man that seemed to love his dog would neglect and then abandon him.

Kevin stared at his feet for what seemed like a long time before he raised his head. Tears ran down his gaunt cheeks as he cleared his throat and tried to speak. After a moment, he regained his voice and told his reasons, stopping often to swallow and work to control his emotions.

"I got King when he was six weeks old. He was a really cute and smart puppy and I had a lot of fun playing with him   and teaching him tricks. Some friends and I shared a rent house in Shreveport that had a big fenced yard. I had a good job as an apprentice cabinetmaker and a nice car. But, I lost my job when the company shut down and nobody else would hire me. I didn't have enough experience, and no one wanted to train me."

Robert watched as Bear licked Kevin's hand and butted his head underneath for a scratch behind the ears. He experienced a twinge of jealousy that changed into sympathy as Kevin continued.

"Without my job, I couldn't pay my car note or my rent. My friends tried to let me stay, but without my share, they didn't have enough to cover the rent. They had to ask me to leave, so I lived in my car until the repo man showed up to tow it away."

Noah opened his mouth as if to ask a question, but thought better of it. He motioned for the young man to go on with his story.

"At first I lived on the streets in Shreveport and panhandled. I even visited a couple of shelters, but they wouldn't let me bring King in. After a while, I got the idea to move to a smaller town with woods, like this one. We stayed in vacant hunting cabins or camped under the stars for a while. It wasn't too bad when I caught fish or found wild berries. After a while, though, I realized we didn't have enough food for both of us to eat. When I saw how thin King had gotten, I decided I had to give him up. I can't even get enough food for myself most days; so I definitely couldn't find enough for him too. A grocery store seemed like a good place to leave him, since there would be plenty of people around. I'm glad he has a good home now."

"You can come home with me," Robert offered. "My mom would feed you and I bet she would help you find a job. She's the police chief and knows lots of people."

Kevin shook his head, sadness radiating from him as he stroked Bear's head.

"No, thanks. I'm not fit to stay in anyone's house right now. Besides, I heard about a company in Oklahoma that's hiring men for the oil fields. I think I'll hitch a ride up there and check it out. Not too many people would give a ride to someone with a Rottweiler."

Noah reached into his back pocket and pulled out his wallet. He extracted several bills and handed them to the young vagrant. When Kevin tried to refuse, Noah took his hand and placed the money in it, wrapping his own fingers around Kevin's.

"Listen to me. Get a shower and some clean clothes. Buy a bus ticket and some food. You'll have a better chance at getting a job if you don't appear like you're homeless."

"But I am homeless, at least right now."

"Yeah, but you don't have to *look* homeless. Come on, take the money. You'll make me feel better."

With that, Kevin laughed and slid the money into his pocket.

"Okay, you win."

He turned to Robert and put out his hand.

"Take good care of Bear, okay?"

Robert noticed he used the dog's new name and swallowed hard against the tears that threatened. One tear escaped and trailed down his cheek when Kevin leaned over to capture Bear's head in his hands and the big dog whined and licked his face.

"Stay here, boy. This is your new home now. You're a great dog and I'm sure going to miss you."

Kevin straightened and gave a brief wave.

"I guess I better get going to buy some clothes and get a motel room where I can take a shower. Thanks for everything."

When Kevin was a few yards away, Bear whined and trotted after his first owner. Robert wanted to call him back, but the lump in his throat prevented any sound from escaping.

Kevin glanced back and stopped. He turned and held up his hand to halt the dog's progress.

"No, Bear. Stay with Robert."

Bear lay on the grass and rested his head on his paws. He whined again, but did not follow Kevin. Robert knelt next to the big dog and wrapped his arms around him, tears running down his cheeks. He was sorry Kevin had to leave Bear when it was obvious he still loved the dog.

But he was so glad Bear was staying.

Noah stood observing the touching scene, a lump in his own throat. He admired Kevin's courage in striking out to search for a job in Oklahoma and hoped the young man would succeed.

He was glad that Robert did not have to lose Bear, though he sympathized with the young vagrant's loss of his canine friend. The boy's love for the big dog was obvious, and Noah didn't want to see his son hurt.

Robert knelt next to Bear with his arms around the Rottweiler, and Noah waited a few minutes before he stepped to his side and laid a comforting hand on his shoulder. Noah wished he had the right to envelop the boy in a hug, but didn't want to push his luck.

"Are you okay, Robert?"

The youngster stood and swiped the tears from his cheeks. He took a deep breath and tried to appear cheerful, but the slight tremble in his chin betrayed his deep feelings.

"Yeah, I'm okay. I sure am glad Kevin told Bear to stay with me. This dog is my best friend."

Noah caught a hint of a sob in Robert's voice, but didn't want to embarrass him by offering too much sympathy. Before he decided what to do next, Robert called Bear to him and picked up the Frisbee.

"I guess we better leave now. It's time for me to go home and do a few chores before dinner. Thanks for coming to help Kevin. It was nice for you to give him that money."

Noah didn't want this brief contact with his son to end, so he turned his steps to walk next to Robert and Bear.

"Do you mind if I walk with you a bit? It's time for me to head back to my hotel room and decide what to have for my dinner. I've been working hard today and worked up an appetite."

"What kind of work do you do?"

Noah described his accounting work, but stopped when he saw Robert's eyes glaze over. Accounting is not everyone's cup of tea, he thought with amusement as Robert yawned while trying to show polite interest. He changed the subject to something he knew the boy was interested in.

"How are you coming with your black belt test?"

Robert brightened.

"It's going great! I'm almost done with my essay and Master Kennedy says I can do the mile run next week. There are a couple more tests, then I'll get my black belt. Mom says she'll throw a party to celebrate."

Noah chuckled at the boy's exuberance. He hungered to be part of the celebration, but couldn't think of a way to get invited without sounding obvious. Robert saved him from trying to figure it out.

"Mom said I can invite anyone I want to come. Would you like to come? Will you still be in town?"

His heart leaped at the chance to spend more time with this special young man.

"You bet! I'll be there with bells on."

Robert gave him a funny look, and Noah realized how strange that must have sounded.

"I mean, I will be glad to attend your black belt promotion celebration."

The boy laughed and Bear pranced beside him, his stubby tail wagging. Noah drank it all in, storing the moment in his memories.

Maggie saved the report on her screen and sat back, rubbing her tired eyes.

Too much time on the computer, she thought. Time to shut things down and go home. As she logged off and locked up her desk, Maggie tried to think of what she would fix for dinner. She had forgotten to set something down to thaw last night, so she did not know what to prepare. Though it lacked much in the way of nutrition, frozen pizza sounded pretty good.

Maggie stepped into the front area to wait for the receptionist. Linda finished locking her own desk and the two women walked out the door together, both of them recognizing Robert and Noah at the same time.

"Who is that with Robert? Oh, that's the good-looking man that came in last week, isn't it?"

Maggie barely heard her. Anger clouded her mind, and she felt the muscles in her neck tighten as she clenched her jaw. How dare he come around her son without her supervision?! Maggie knew she *told* him...

She held her temper because of Robert's presence, but Maggie planned to ream Noah out when she got him alone. This time, she would make sure he understood the rules if he wanted to spend any time with Robert.

Noah glanced up just in time to spot Maggie stepping out of the police station and walking their way along with another woman. He recognized the young woman as the receptionist who pointed out Maggie's office his first day in Forrestville.

Noah gave both women a pleasant smile, which faded when he saw Maggie's thunderous expression. Uh oh! The warm emotions experienced as he walked with his son dissipated as he realized his transgression of Maggie's rules could cost him the chance to spend time with the boy. He cast about in his mind for a way to salvage the situation.

Linda's eyes seemed to take it all in, but she went on her way, asking no questions. After she left, Maggie opened her mouth to speak, but Robert jumped in.

"Mom! We found Bear's first owner! He's a homeless guy who couldn't take care of Bear, so he left him at the grocery store. Mr. Jameson gave Kevin, that's the guy, some money to pay for a shower and some clothes and go to Oklahoma to get a job. Bear wanted to go with him, but Kevin told him to stay with me. I sure am glad. If he had gone to Oklahoma with him, I sure would have missed Bear."

The torrent of words from Robert's mouth stopped Maggie, and Noah watched in amusement as she tried to absorb everything the boy had said. He stepped in before she caught her breath.

"I was in the park when Kevin and Robert met and it seemed, uh, wise, for me to introduce myself. After Kevin left, Robert walked with me on my way back to the bed-and-breakfast."

Maggie's expression eased after Noah's explanation. Though she seemed suspicious that he "happened" to be in the park, he recognized when she understood why he felt it wise to introduce himself. Noah knew, however, that she was still unhappy with the fact he had been alone with Robert. Her eyes still snapped, and she had a slight twitch in one eyelid that he bet she didn't know about.

Noah had to stifle a chuckle as he realized something. His ex-wife looked cute when angry! He appreciated she would not find this revelation humorous. He also realized that he had the insane desire to grab her and plant a kiss on her lips, but Noah knew *that* would not end well!

Maggie watched Noah as indiscernible expressions chased across his face. She watched the firm lips she had always loved kissing and wondered what it would be like to be kissed by him again.

What was she thinking?! Maggie was furious with him for disregarding her wishes regarding Robert. She didn't want to feel this renewed attraction toward her ex-husband. In fact, she didn't even want him here.

Yeah, right, Maggie thought. Keep telling yourself that. She knew her heart was softening toward Noah, but he had hurt her in the past, and she did not want to risk being hurt again.

So, she would guard her heart and her son against this man who was so familiar and yet a stranger.

Chapter 9

Maggie watched with satisfaction as townspeople and tourists mingled for Forrestville's Autumn Festival. The aroma of funnel cakes and candy apples hung in the air as children raced from one booth to another. The sound of lambs bleating rose from the petting zoo. It was the most popular attraction at the festival, as children and their parents enjoyed the animals provided by local farmers.

"Mom! Did you see the horses Ms. Kendall brought?"

Robert and his friends clustered around her. The boys were excited about the opportunity to ride under the careful supervision of ranch owner Kendall Ford and a few of the cowhands from the Rocking K ranch. Maggie loved seeing her son having so much fun, but she hoped he didn't ask her for a horse next. A cat and a dog were more than enough for her.

As the boys chattered and boasted about their riding skills, the hairs on Maggie's neck rose. She had the chilling sensation that someone was watching her. A wave of protectiveness surged through her as she thought of danger coming to any of these youngsters. Maggie didn't want to alarm her son and his friends. She only wanted them to be cautious because not every stranger in town was a harmless tourist.

When Maggie heard the group discussing a night time hike in the woods, she issued a firm "absolutely not" to their plans.

"Boys, I'm sorry, but that's not a good idea. We have too many strangers in town for you to be wandering through the woods in the dark."

One boy tried to protest that they would hike, not "wander," but Robert interrupted.

"No, Matt, Mom's right. We're smart enough woodsmen to understand that the woods are dangerous at night. But what if one of the younger kids sees us and tries to follow? One of them might get lost."

The other boys muttered, but agreed to skip the hike. Maggie gave her son a proud, approving look. As the boys walked away debating which booth to visit next, the hairs on Maggie's neck raised again. That sensation of being watched still lingered. She turned from the festivities and sought a quieter area that would allow her to get a better view of the crowd.

Maggie found a corner with no foot traffic and stood, sweeping the downtown area with her eyes. Though a part of her mind took in the festival, her thoughts were in turmoil. Maggie knew Noah wanted a chance to build a relationship with Robert, and she had to admit that he seemed to be a different man. But she had a hard time letting go of the fear of being hurt again. More than that, she didn't want Robert to be hurt. Maggie tried to pray about it, but she couldn't seem to let go of her struggle and trust God to guide her.

Maggie's ears picked up a voice calling her name at the same time she sensed movement to her right. A figure in a black ski mask loomed next to her with his hand raised, a knife gleaming in the streetlights.

Noah sat at a picnic table, trying to figure out how to eat the chili dog in front of him without wearing it. He spotted a box of plastic utensils and grabbed a fork, removing the wrapper.

While he enjoyed his dinner, he observed Maggie talking to Robert and a few of his friends and wondered what she said that caused the grumbling in the small group. Whatever it was, it seemed she and Robert had prevailed. The boys ambled away, pointing at games and booths they wanted to visit.

He took a sip from his soft drink as he kept his eyes on Maggie until she disappeared into the crowd. After providing supervision at the park, when Robert met Bear's first owner, Noah and his ex-wife had an uneasy truce at the moment. She was letting him spend time with Robert under her supervision, under the guise of him visiting with her as an old friend. He hoped to persuade Maggie to tell their son the truth soon, but first Noah had to show Maggie he was not the drug and alcohol addict she had left.

Noah's train of thought diverted as a strong sense of uneasiness welled up inside him. Something was wrong, but he didn't know what. Noah wished Cy was here. His friend had gone back to Shreveport for the weekend to help his church with their Fall Festival. Now Noah wished for Cy's imposing presence.

He got up from the table, his half-eaten chili dog forgotten. Noah had an overwhelming sense that Maggie was in danger. It didn't matter that she was a seasoned police officer trained in self-defense. An urgency to find her gnawed at him, even if he didn't know what to after that.

Noah found his ex-wife standing in a quiet area, scanning the crowds. Her loveliness struck him again. No longer the fresh innocence of the young girl he had fallen in love with all those years ago, now Maggie had the mature beauty of someone who had encountered hard times and risen above them. Attraction stirred inside him, but he had to wonder if there was more to it than physical desire. Was he still in love with her?

As the questions circled in his mind, Noah saw a dark form detach itself from the shadows and approach Maggie, a knife raised high above her head. A warning cry burst from his mouth as Noah ran toward her with a speed he didn't realize he possessed.

Maggie swung around and backpedaled from the assailant, avoiding the slash of the gleaming blade. She stumbled over a piece of rough sidewalk and fell, landing on her back. When the figure stood over her and raised an arm to try again, she lashed out with a booted foot, catching her attacker on the knee. The hooded figure roared a deep, guttural howl of pain.

Noah arrived in time to tackle the assailant, knocking the knife out of the big man's hand and across the sidewalk. He wrestled him to the ground and tried to pin him down, but the attacker got a hand free and punched Noah in the jaw. Noah's hold loosened as he fought the pain and dizziness and the man pushed Noah off of him and staggered to his feet, snatching up the knife and limping into the shadows. Though Maggie called out for the man to stop, the attacker had already gotten away.

"Noah! Are you all right?"

Maggie helped him sit up, wincing at the swelling Noah knew had started in his face. He peered into her blue eyes that warmed with sympathy and something else. Gratitude? Attraction? Before he could pursue the thought, Maggie stood and extended a hand to help him up. He flashed a smile, though it hurt like crazy.

"Thanks. I'll have a doozy of a bruise, but I think I'm okay."

Noah rubbed his jaw as he struggled to his feet. He was not sure the danger to Maggie was past, and he preferred to face any potential attacks on his feet.

Maggie stepped back and stared into the shadows where the attacker had disappeared. Her mouth flattened into a hard line.

"That's two attacks and a break-in," she muttered.

Noah's head snapped around at her words.

"What? He's attacked you before?"

Maggie's expression showed she regretted saying the words. She sighed as she turned to answer him.

"Yes, he's the reason I have a cat now."

"Huh?"

What did a cat have to do with her being attacked?

Maggie chuckled, and the sound of her laughter broke the tension. She explained about the attack in the alley and how the assailant had used a half-grown cat as a weapon. She also described the attempted break-in and Bear's part in stopping the intruder.

Rage built inside Noah. Though Maggie knew how to defend herself, Noah still had an attitude of protectiveness toward her.

"Maggie, what is this guy up to? Is he stalking you?"

She nodded, her expression sobering.

"I've had the same thought. I need to check into recent prison releases for anyone who would have a reason to come after me."

Noah pondered Maggie's words as they rejoined the festival crowds. He had never considered the dangers she faced as a police officer. During their marriage, he was on drugs, so her job was nothing more than an inconvenience to him, but now, he realized what she risked protecting others. Pride and gratitude welled up in him, as well as concern for her safety. Even good cops got hurt or killed in the line of duty.

When they got to the picnic tables, he waved off Maggie's offer to summon an EMT. She stared at him for a moment before leaving to get a bag of ice for his aching jaw. Noah watched her as she hurried toward the concession stands.

"Mr. Jameson, what happened?"

Robert stood in front of him, concern darkening his blue eyes.

"I'm okay, son. Just got decked by someone who… wanted to fight. I scared him off though."

Noah knew Maggie would not want him to tell this young boy that someone tried to kill his mother. At the boy's dubious look, he realized his story sounded ludicrous. Though trim and fit, Noah was not a big or muscular man. He treated it like a joke.

"Yeah, I threatened to tell him about my stamp collection. He ran away screaming. Didn't you hear him?"

Robert laughed and turned toward Maggie as she brought the ice pack.

"Did you see the fight, Mom? Did you see the guy try to fight Mr. Jameson?"

Maggie looked at her ex-husband and her son. She had overheard the joke Noah made and appreciated that he did not tell Robert the actual story. When she glanced at Noah, he winked at her. As she tried not to blush, Maggie turned to her son and laughed.

"I sure did. I almost arrested Mr. Jameson for threatening the man with such a dire punishment."

After Robert ran back to join his friends, Maggie and

Noah sat in a comfortable silence. Noah moved the ice pack off his jaw and caught Maggie's eye. Before he said anything, she spoke up.

"I'm still not sure about you, Noah. But you attacked the man who attempted to kill me and tried to capture him."

Noah had to wince at the words "tried to' as he experienced a frustrating sense of failure that the attacker got away. His thoughts wandered, wondering what would happen next. He realized Maggie still had something to say and turned his attention back to her.

"I also appreciate that you didn't tell Robert about the attack."

He nodded once, not sure of what to say. She had a dangerous job, and Robert was smart enough to understand it. But that didn't mean the boy needed to know about every time someone threatened his mother's life.

Mickey limped down the quiet streets and into the woods surrounding Forrestville. Rage overcame him as he leaned against a tree and swore, using every cuss word in his vocabulary.

He almost had her. A few more inches and his knife would have taken her out. Then that fool came barging in, yelling and warning his target. What business was it of his, anyway? If the meddler hadn't warned her, Maggie Jones would not have seen him in time to back away. And she would not have been able to kick him in the knee.

Mickey swore again as he reached to rub where she got him. He hoped Maggie's powerful kick didn't break or dislocate his kneecap. Mickey flexed and straightened his leg a few times, grimacing at the soreness. Anyway, the fact he'd been able to get away might be a good sign she didn't break anything.

He glared at the small town as if it were to blame for his troubles, then turned to hike to the campsite. As he hobbled along, Mickey tried to plan what to do next, but he burned with frustration. Three attempts to kill that woman and three times something got in the way.

First, the attack in the alley. Mickey grinned at his idea to use the cat to distract Maggie. With her hands full of yowling cat, he should have been able to cut her throat and get out of the alley before anyone caught on to what happened. Instead, that woman from the bakery chose that moment to come outside to see what was happening. He barely escaped before the woman saw him.

The break-in at the police chief's house also should have been easy. Get in, cut her throat while she slept, and get out. Who knew she owned that monster that looked like a bear? The big mutt scared the daylights out of him when he opened the window (though he would never admit his fear to anyone else). It was the dog's fault he dropped his favorite knife and had to run for his life. He still broke out in goosebumps when he recalled how close those sharp teeth had come to his skin.

Mickey blew out a breath as he approached the little hunting shack. He hated any kind of failure. Failing to kill his enemy angered him most. But he would make Maggie Jones pay for ruining his life. Somehow, she would pay.

"I don't have all day, woman!"

Maggie looked up from her shopping list at the sound of the belligerent voice from the front of the store. She eased toward the end of the aisle and peeked around the corner, hoping she would not need to get involved in an altercation.

A grizzled, heavyset man stood at the checkout, glaring at the flustered cashier who was trying to ring up his items and bag at the same time. She dropped a can of beans and bent to pick it up. When she stood up, the disgruntled customer snatched the can from her hand and stuffed it in the bag, which he grabbed from in front of her. He slammed a handful of bills on the counter. When the clerk picked them up in a trembling hand and attempted to work the cash register to get the man's change, he waved her off with an impatient hand and strode toward the door.

"Ferget it!"

Maggie thought about intervening, but observed Emma approaching the tearful cashier. She watched as the store owner spoke a few quiet words to her employee and pointed toward the back. Maggie guessed she was telling the distraught woman to take a break.

With a full cart and her list completed, Maggie headed for the checkout. Emma manned it herself, and Maggie could see she was fuming about the rudeness of the now-departed customer.

"Can you believe that man?!"

Maggie put the first item on the conveyor belt and shook her head in sympathy as she emptied her cart. The store owner rang up each item with a little more force than was necessary. Emma still had plenty to say about the man and his treatment of her cashier, and she punctuated every few words with a forceful push on the cash register keys.

"**That** is the **rudest** creature I have **ever** met! **Just** because **poor** Natalie couldn't move **fast** enough to **suit** him, he about **bit** her head off."

Maggie swept the front area with her eyes, searching

for the teenager who bagged for the store. When she didn't spot him, she interrupted Emma.

"Where's Charlie?"

Emma stopped for a breath before jumping right back into her tirade.

"Charlie had to quit because he graduated early, and he's starting at Louisiana State University in Shreveport. Now I'm without a bagger, and taking care of the store is wearing Natalie and me to a frazzle. I have to say, people like **that** man don't help at all!"

While Emma went on about how busy they had been and how tired they were, Maggie stepped toward the front of the store and gazed through the windows, searching for the object of Emma's wrath.

Maggie watched the heavyset man as he shambled out of the parking lot and turned left, favoring his right knee as he moved toward the trees. As she tried to figure out why he looked familiar, Maggie remembered the man who stuck his head in the nail salon a few days earlier. She was almost sure the offensive customer was the same man. But there was something else about the way he moved; especially the limp. Maggie wondered if it was from a recent injury or if he'd always had it.

"Emma, do you know who that man is? He's not a local."

The store owner pursed her lips and gave an emphatic shake of her head, her hazel eyes still snapping with outrage.

"He just started coming in here a couple of weeks ago. He never smiles or says 'Hello.' He gets a few items, slaps the money on the counter, and grunts like a pig! I wish he would take his business elsewhere."

Maggie listened to Emma's rant as she paid for her purchases and wondered about the stranger. After his abrupt and unsettling visit to the nail salon, she had checked around town, but no one could tell her who he was or where he was staying.

Something about him put Maggie on edge.

Noah browsed the knife counter, stopping to admire a small dagger in a leather sheath. He spotted a couple of throwing stars and wondered if Robert would ever train with something like those. Maybe he would when he was older and more advanced in his training. Noah didn't know if martial arts schools even taught students how to use weapons like those.

When he spotted the specialty shirts and caps, Noah moved to check them out. He considered buying one for Robert, but hesitated. Would Maggie allow him to give Robert a gift like that? Would it cause trouble between them?

Maggie and Noah had a tentative truce between them since the attack at the Fall Festival. Noah understood Maggie felt gratitude for his part in interrupting the thug's attempt on her life. She had also told him she appreciated his not telling Robert about the attack. Noah believed he was making progress in making amends to his ex-wife.

"Hi Alex! I came to check out the new .22's you told me about. I don't know if I can get one, but it sure would make a great Christmas present for Robert. I'll have to look at what you have and what the price is."

Noah's head snapped up at the sound of Maggie's voice. Without knowing why, he moved to the other side of the shirt rack, where he could hear the conversation without being seen. He experienced a small amount of guilt for eavesdropping, but continued to hide and listen anyway.

Alexander Starr, known to his customers as Alex, grinned at the police chief and stepped to a display case, which he unlocked and reached into. He pulled out a fine-looking .22 rifle and laid it with care on the top of the glass case.

Maggie moved to get a closer look at the gun, picking it up and turning it around as she examined it, then laying it with care in the same place on the counter. Noah noticed the glint of admiration in her eyes as her hands caressed the stock.

"How much?"

Noah watched through the shirts as the gun shop owner quoted a price that made Maggie's eye widen and her hand jerk away from the weapon. It didn't seem all that expensive too him, but Maggie's expression made him realize it might be too much for her.

When he stopped to reflect about it, Noah realized Maggie, in all likelihood, didn't make a large salary being the police chief of a small town. She probably earned enough to pay the bills and buy their necessities, but not much more.

"I'll have a gun safety class for kids right after the New Year. It's half-price if you get the gun from here."

Alex picked up the rifle and held it out temptingly for Maggie, his dark face creased in a mischievous grin. The twinkle in his eye showed he was aware Maggie wanted to buy that rifle for her son and he was going to do his best to sell it to her before she walked out of the shop.

Maggie took the rifle from his hands again, her eyes gleaming at its quality. After admiring it for a moment, she handed it back to him with a smile and a sigh.

"Let me think about it, okay? It's a good price, but I have to consider a few things."

Alex's grin dropped for a moment, then he tried again.

"Now chief, you know that boy is old enough and responsible enough for this gun. I had a gun when I was younger than he is. Took good care of that rifle and brought home dinner many a time."

She just thanked him and turned away. After she left the shop, Noah stepped out from behind the shirts and watched Maggie through the window. She stood a few yards down, chatting with a couple of the old men lounging outside. He declined Alex's offer to help him and hurried out the door to catch up with her.

"Maggie!"

Noah almost ran the last few steps to stand beside his ex-wife. His calves burned with tension at the quick jog and reminded him of his need for more exercise. Noah turned his attention to Maggie as he considered how to make his offer. In the end, he simply blurted it out.

"Can I help you buy that rifle for Robert?"

Wow, Noah, that was smooth, he thought. She'd know he was eavesdropping and suspect him and his offer.

Sure enough, her expression turned stormy as she turned a hot glare on him.

"How do you know about the rifle? Were you spying on me?"

Noah bristled.

"Why would I want to spy on you, woman? Don't be so paranoid. I was looking around in the gun shop when you came in. I saw the rifle he showed you and thought it would be nice if I could help you buy it for our son. But if you don't want my help, never mind!"

He wheeled around and stomped away, his face and neck red. Noah realized his behavior was childish, but the anger and hurt at her suspicions had seized his thoughts.

He was tired of her grudges and doubts about him, even after he saved her life.

"Noah, wait!"

He stopped, but did not turn around as Maggie hurried to join him. If she planned to ream him out, he wasn't sure he could hold on to his temper. Though his jaw ached from clenching his teeth, Noah didn't want to say something that would destroy the fragile peace between them.

"I'm sorry I accused you."

Noah turned, his eyes wide at her unexpected apology. He gave a brief nod and waited.

"I'm just not sure I'm ready yet for us to give him a joint gift like that. He still doesn't know, um, you know."

"He doesn't know I'm his father."

Maggie glanced around, but stopped short of shushing him, though Noah could see she wanted to ask him to keep his voice down. His heart cramped knowing she didn't want anyone to know about their relationship. He understood why she hid the information, but it still hurt.

"Okay, I'll stay out of it."

"Noah, I'm sorry. Just, give me some time, okay? I understand I have to tell him, but, well, it's hard. He's going to be so upset that I lied to him."

Maggie looked down at her hands as she spoke, her voice low and distressed. Regret and sorrow washed over him. If he had been the right kind of husband and father, she would not have left him and felt the need to lie to their son about his father. He reached to touch her, but dropped his hand to his side. Noah waited until Maggie looked up again.

"It's okay, Mags, really. I understand and I'll do whatever I can to help."

Chapter 10

Robert riffled through the documents in his mother's box of important papers. His friends at school didn't believe that he got his green belt when he was ten, so he wanted to find the certificate to show them. He cast a furtive glance behind him to make sure he was alone. His mom hadn't said for him to stay out of the box, but she kept it tucked in a corner of a shelf in her closet. Robert suspected she would not like him digging through it.

He spied the corner of his promotion certificate and pulled it out with a crow of triumph. Now he could show the guys. As he tugged the colored paper out, several other documents spilled from the box, including a photograph that slid out of the pile and landed on the floor.

Curious, Robert set down his promotion certificate and sifted through the scattered papers. He found a marriage certificate, a divorce decree, and a birth certificate, which was his. Robert's eyes widened as he took in the names on the marriage and divorce papers; then he checked the dates on the divorce decree and on his birth certificate. He was born about seven months after the date on the divorce paperwork.

Robert lifted the 8x10 photograph from the floor and studied it for a long moment. The picture showed a young couple in wedding clothes. They looked so happy as they held hands and smiled at the photographer that they reminded him of Jesse and Rachel when they got married.

Robert inspected the couple and with a jolt, recognized his mother. She'd told him his father died when he was a baby, but he couldn't imagine his mother as a married woman. The groom also seemed familiar, as if Robert had met him somewhere. The boy's hands trembled when he realized why. He knew this man!

He gathered the documents and the photograph under his arm and put the rest of the papers in the box, which he arranged in its original resting place. When he finished, he backed out of the closet and sat on his mother's bed. What did this mean?

The boy bit his lip as he tried not to cry. He'd ask his mom when she got home. She'd told him his dad was dead. She wouldn't lie to him, would she?

"Robert, I'm home!"

Maggie set her purse in a chair and sorted through the mail in her hand. She set the bills on her desk in the living room and threw away the circulars. It was less than half-way through November, and the pile of Christmas junk mail in her box seemed to grow every day.

She glanced toward Robert's room and noticed his door was closed. He must be studying, she assumed. Her son was an excellent student, making almost straight A's, as well as studying for his black belt test. She decided to leave him alone while she started on dinner.

Maggie turned toward the kitchen and gathered the ingredients for brownies to go with the spaghetti and salad they were having for dinner. Noah was coming for a "visit from an old friend." Though she knew she had to do it, Maggie dreaded the day she had to tell her son the truth she'd been hiding from him.

Just as she was ready to pour the batter into the pan, she heard her son's voice.

"Mom, is Mr. Jameson my father?"

Maggie jumped and dropped the bowl. Although it didn't break, the batter splattered out of it all over the kitchen floor.

"Robert! You scared me!"

She knelt to clean up the mess, glad to have a moment to gather her thoughts. When she stood again and glanced at Robert's determined face, Maggie's heart sank. This was not the time she had wanted to have this discussion. She stood with the bowl in her shaking hands and placed it with great care on the counter, taking a deep breath to stave off the tremors in her voice before answering her son.

"What makes you think he's your father?"

Robert spread out the documents and the photograph on the kitchen table and pointed an accusing finger at them.

"That's you and Mr. Jameson when you were younger, isn't it? You were married to him, then you divorced him, SEVEN MONTHS BEFORE I WAS BORN! Why did you tell me my father was dead?"

Maggie slumped and closed her eyes. She didn't even have the heart or the energy to chastise her son for getting into her important papers. How could she explain this?

"It's complicated, son."

Robert stared at her, a scowl marring his pleasant features. The dimple he inherited from Noah was not peeking out now. Maggie studied the tracks of recent tears on his face and her heart hurt, knowing she caused his grief.

"Mom, you told me to always be honest with you. You

told me we always had to tell each other the truth, even when it was not convenient or might get us in trouble."

Maggie tried to interrupt to explain, but Robert wouldn't listen. Tears ran down his furious young face.

"You lied to me! All my life you've been lying to me! You told me my father was dead, but you lied!"

With that, Robert whirled and ran out the kitchen door, slamming it behind him. Bear trotted to the middle of the kitchen and stood, quivering between consoling Maggie, who was sobbing, or following his boy, who was hurting. He turned mournful eyes toward Maggie. She wiped her eyes and moved to open the door.

"Go with him, boy. He needs you now."

The Rottweiler licked her hand and bounded out the door. Maggie watched as the dog caught up with Robert and the two headed into her son's favorite place, the woods.

"What's going on here?"

Maggie turned at the sound of Noah's voice. Tears ran down her lovely face as she wrapped her arms around her waist.

"Maggie?"

Alarm filled Noah as he observed her posture. He had never seen Maggie this broken, not even when their marriage ended. Without considering the consequences, he enveloped her in a hug. She stiffened, then laid her head on his shoulder and sobbed. Noah held his ex-wife and rubbed her back in soothing circles, his thoughts whirling as he sought to understand her grief.

After a moment, she took a deep breath and stepped back from him. Noah kept a hand on her arm until he was sure she was steady on her feet. Maggie looked up at him with anguished eyes.

"He knows."

Resentment stirred in Noah's mind.

"Maggie, I had hoped we would tell him together. I understand you still don't trust me, but…"

"I didn't tell him. He found papers and a photograph and figured it out for himself. Now he will never trust me again."

"I can't believe you told him his father was dead."

Maggie glared at him.

"It was better than telling him you didn't want him. That you wanted me to abort him because you were too busy partying, boozing, and getting high!"

Noah closed his eyes as Maggie reminded him of a past he wanted to forget. The tentacles of shame and regret that writhed within threatened to choke him as he stumbled to a chair and slumped into it. Tears stung his eyes as he held his head in his hands. All Noah could think about was how much he missed because he chose liquor and drugs over his wife and son. No wonder Maggie felt the need to lie to Robert about his father. The boy deserved better than a drunk and an addict.

"I'm sorry."

He spoke the words so softly he wasn't sure Maggie heard, but when he raised his head, he found her staring at him with a strange expression of anger mixed with compassion.

Maggie walked to the window to peer out into the backyard. Dusk was falling and Noah saw the worry on her face. As she wiped more tears from her cheeks, two shadows entered the yard through the back gate. With a sigh of relief, Maggie turned to her ex-husband.

"Noah, we can't tell Robert you wanted me to abort

him. You can tell him about your past if you think that's best, but DO NOT tell him you wanted me to abort."

"Maggie, I know better than that."

He stopped at her look that reminded him how incredibly stupid he had been in the past. He gazed into her eyes for a long moment, then nodded.

Robert came through the back door and averted his eyes when he saw Maggie and Noah standing together, waiting for him. The dog squeezed in past him and trotted to his food bowl. He sniffed the empty bowl and gazed at Robert with a hungry, expectant expression. The boy poured the dry kibble into the container without saying a word.

He did not look at his parents until he had put away the bag of dog food and refilled the water bowl. It reached the point Noah could not stand the silence for another minute before Robert spoke.

"How long did you know about me?"

He pinned Noah with an accusing stare, his blue eyes swollen and red from crying.

"Why didn't you ever come see me, or at least write to me? I'm twelve years old and I never even knew about you until today!"

Noah gestured toward the kitchen table, where the documents and pictures were still spread.

"Son, let's sit down and talk about this. There are some things you should understand about me, things I did that I'm not proud of."

"No! You don't get to call me son! You've never even been here for me!"

Noah sucked in a breath at the hurt Robert's words

caused. The boy was right, though. He didn't deserve to call this young man his son. He tried again.

"You're right. I don't deserve it. But you deserve to hear why I wasn't here. Please, can we sit down while I explain?"

The boy hesitated, then pulled out a chair and slumped into it. He shot a defiant glance at Maggie and Noah as they settled in their chairs. Robert looked down at the birth certificate in front of him, picking it up to study it, then his parents' divorce decree. Noah's heart clenched as his son scrubbed a fist across his eyes, as if fighting tears.

"Robert, look at me."

Robert gave him a brief, hostile glance, then looked down at the table again. After a long pause, he lifted his gaze to rest on his father's face. Noah blinked back his own tears and tried to take a deep breath. He tried to think of the best way to explain to his son why he had not been a part of the boy's life.

"I have to tell you why I never came to see you or called you or wrote to you."

At Maggie's quick, indrawn breath, Noah shot her a reassuring glance and continued.

"Son, I mean Robert, I wasn't worthy to be your father or to have any part in your life. I was a cold, selfish drug addict and alcoholic who only cared about myself and the next high or drink out there. Your mother wanted to protect you from me, and she was right."

"Are you still a drug addict or alcoholic?"

Noah smiled at his son.

"No, several years ago, I met the Lord Jesus. He helped me get off the drugs and alcohol by introducing me to a group of men who stood by me and held me accountable. I haven't taken a drink or had any drugs in over five years."

Maggie remembered how she had judged him because

she discovered him standing in front of the Pot O' Gold bar with his friend. She realized she might have been too hasty to jump to conclusions, but still harbored reservations about trusting him. She turned her attention back to their conversation.

"But you didn't even try!"

Robert was crying again. Maggie experienced a fierce desire to wrap him up in her arms and protect him, but she realized she couldn't protect him from this hurt.

Noah glanced at Maggie, then back at their son. It already upset the boy that his mother had lied to him about his father being dead. He would not tell this hurting child that his father had wanted him aborted.

"Remember, I said I was cold and selfish?"

Robert nodded.

"I wasn't aware when you were born because I was in a haze of alcohol and drugs. In fact, right before she left me, I even tried to hit your mother."

Noah stopped, his eyes taking on a far-away glaze as he remembered when Maggie told him she was leaving him.

"No, Maggie, I do not want to go to church with you!"

Noah looked up at his wife from the couch, a scowl creasing his face. Several months earlier, Maggie had attended a women's event at her friend Monica's church. She had returned with her face glowing and kept talking about how God had forgiven her sins and could forgive his sins too. Noah didn't think he and Maggie were such great sinners. When he tried to tell her that, she just lectured him on the Bible and everyone being a sinner. Now she attended church every chance she got and talked about Jesus until he thought he would go out of his mind.

He sighed, feeling sorry for himself. His wife was a

pregnant religious fanatic and a cop. She never wanted to go to parties with him anymore. She always gave him dirty looks when she caught him drinking a beer or some other alcoholic drink. Noah snickered as he decided to show her something "special." He fished in his pocket and pulled out a small cellophane bag. Pouring its contents onto the coffee table, he prepared for his next fix.

Maggie stood as if in shock with a horrified expression on her pretty face.

"Noah, are you out of your mind?! What are you doing with that stuff?"

Noah only grinned at her outrage. His grin disappeared, however, when Maggie swept the fine white powder off the table. He lurched to his feet, his face red with anger.

"How dare you?!"

He got up in her face, breathing hard. She met his gaze with a hard, unflinching stare of her own. No longer did he see the soft, loving regard in her beautiful blue eyes. Now they had nothing but contempt for him. It made him even angrier. And before he considered what he was doing, he raised his hand to slap her.

Noah never touched her. Maggie grabbed his wrist and whirled him around, twisting his arm behind him. He yelled and struggled for a couple of minutes before he stilled. He remembered from past discussions with his wife that struggling only made it worse.

She released him with a shove away from her, and he plopped back onto the couch, still seething at the loss of his cocaine. His wife's eyes regarded him with that mixture of love, pity, and hurt he had recognized a lot in the past few months.

Noah glimpsed himself on the television's screen. His unwashed hair hung in limp strands around his acne-scarred *face. The shirt he was wearing was wrinkled and stained. It didn't matter. As long as he looked good when he went out, he didn't care what he looked like at home.*

He heard what sounded like a sob as Maggie turned away for a moment. When she turned back, however, all he saw from her was cold self-control.

"Noah, I'm leaving you. I can put up with a lot and I have for the past year. But I will not become your punching bag. Our marriage is over and I want nothing from you. Just, just stay away from me."

Noah blinked at her words. Maggie was leaving him? He thought about protesting because there was still a part of him that loved her. But he reconsidered and let her go. He had more important things to think about, like where to get more cocaine.

The memory sent chills down his spine as he remembered how close he came to striking Maggie. Noah drew in a deep breath so he could continue.

"Thank God, I never got the chance again to hurt her. She left me that day and she was right to do so. Your mother kept you away from me for your protection because of the man I had become. I understand that you're angry and hurt. You feel like your mother betrayed you by not telling you the truth about me, don't you?"

Robert shot Maggie an angry glance.

"Yes. She should have told me!"

"Robert, I won't say it was right for your mother to lie to you. But you realize she did it because she loves you, right?"

Robert hesitated. He looked at his mother, who sat across the table from him with tears running down her face. Noah watched the boy struggling to understand the love that made Maggie try to protect him with a lie.

"Yeah, I can understand she was trying to protect me."

Robert turned his attention to his mother. It was obvious the boy still hurt when his voice wobbled as he spoke to her.

"Mom, I want to forgive you because that's what a Christian should do. But, I don't feel like I can trust you anymore."

Noah heard a small gasp from Maggie, but when he leaned forward as if he would intervene, she noticed the move and gave a slight shake of her head. He understood she needed him to back off as Robert continued.

"You always told me we had to be open and honest with each other, but you weren't telling me the truth all this time. How can I believe anything you say after this big lie?"

Before Maggie could respond, Robert got up and moved toward his room. Maggie followed him a few steps, before she hesitated and told him it was almost time for dinner.

"I'm not hungry. Just leave me alone, okay? I need to think."

Noah and Maggie watched him stride to his room, the big Rottweiler close behind him. After the boy closed his bedroom door, Noah turned to Maggie.

"You okay?"

Maggie's sobs had stopped, but the hurt and guilt on her face broke Noah's heart, especially when she spoke.

"I've lost my son's trust. I don't know if I'll ever be okay again."

Chapter 11

Robert unlocked the front door and pushed through, dumping his school backpack on the floor. He took a few steps toward the kitchen for a snack, then stopped as if he could hear his mother's voice telling him to pick up the backpack and put it in his room. In an unwonted act of defiance, Robert left it where he dropped it.

He almost made it to the kitchen door when the guilt hit. Resistance lasted almost a minute before he returned to the small foyer with a martyr-like sigh and picked up the offending item, yanking it onto his shoulder by one strap. He muttered about how unfair his mother was to make him put things away all the time as he trudged back to his room.

After depositing the heavy bag on his bed, the boy turned again toward the kitchen. He was hungry after studying all day. Somehow, it seemed a long time since lunch.

Robert rummaged through the pantry and cabinets, but found nothing that appealed. Granola bars and fruit just didn't seem satisfying. He closed the cabinet door and stood, wondering if Zach was at the cabin and if he was roasting wieners today. The memory of those tasty sausages made the hungry boy's stomach rumble.

Robert decided he wanted to go for a hike and go by the hunting cabin to find Zach. *Maybe* his new friend would be outside cooking and Robert could get a hot dog.

After locking the back door, Robert strode through the yard and out the back gate, taking the well-worn path through the woods. This was Robert's favorite place to hike. He enjoyed watching the leaves on the trees change colors and drop and the silence that surrounded him, broken only by the crunch of leaves under his feet, the calls of birds or the rustle of squirrels dashing for the trees.

As he walked, Robert thought about the events of the past few weeks. So much had happened! He tried to put it in order: finding Bear (Boy; he missed Bear! It would sure be nice when his friend got back from the vet), Sensei Kennedy telling him he was ready to test for his black belt. Oh yeah, he needed to study some more for that tonight. Anyway, what else? Meeting Mr. Jameson, Mom bringing home the cat.

He paused. He could not ignore the event that loomed largest in his mind - learning that his mother had been lying to him about his father's death and finding out Mr. Jameson was his father.

Robert still struggled with why his father had nothing to do with him until now. He could kind of understand that Mr. Jameson had been addicted to drugs and alcohol, but it still seemed as if...

And Mom lying to him! That hurt the most. Sure, she was protecting him. He got that. But it just made no sense she lied to him after the way she always harped on him about telling the truth.

Robert had told her he forgave her, but he knew he had been pretty cold to her since that night. His conscience twinged when he remembered the hurt look on her face this morning when he left for school without kissing her goodbye. And she looked like she was getting sick, too. She'd been coughing all morning and sounded pretty hoarse.

"Jesus forgave you, so you must forgive others."

His Sunday School teacher's voice echoed in his head. They were studying about forgiveness at church. Robert believed he forgave others - most of the time. He had even forgiven that smart-mouth kid who ragged him about not having a father. Of course, if Robert were honest about it, he *had* put the kid in a pretty painful hold for a couple of minutes. But afterward, he and the kid had gone hiking with the others and everything had been cool between them.

"I'll forgive her," he said out loud. "But, I just don't trust her."

Is that forgiving?

Robert shook his head as he tramped through the woods. He didn't want to think about forgiving anymore. He wanted to set it all aside and enjoy his hike. Pretty soon it would be too cold to be walking through the woods and his mom would tell him to hold off until Spring. More of Mom being protective.

With that, he picked up a stick and began working his way through the drills for the bo. He had almost finished when the scent of roasting sausages teased his nostrils. Robert threw down the stick and stepped into the clearing where his new friend Zach sat by a fire.

"Hi Zach! How's it goin'?"

Zach looked up as Robert stepped over the log next to the fire and sat down next to him. He grinned at the

boy as he eyed Zach's hot dog. Funny how this kid always showed up while he was roasting wieners. Of course, he did roast hot dogs a lot. They were cheap and easy to fix.

Zach handed his stick to Robert and reached for another sausage, which he slid onto a skewer and gave to Robert. He took his stick back and tested the wiener to see if it was hot enough. Satisfied, he enveloped it in a bun and doused it with a generous portion of mustard.

"Where's the dog?" he mumbled through a mouthful. Zach looked around, as if expecting Bear to materialize in the woods.

"Oh, he had to go to the vet's today."

"What's wrong with him?"

"Nothing. He just had to get his teeth cleaned."

Zach drew back and stared at Robert.

"What? Why does a dog need his teeth cleaned?"

When he saw Robert glance at his mouth, Zach wanted to cover it or turn his head away. He knew his own teeth looked terrible. They were yellow and dingy and he was missing a couple. Somehow he never got around to taking care of them, other than brushing them occasionally. He forced himself to not turn away and to keep his attention on Robert as he explained why Bear needed his teeth cleaned.

"His teeth and gums had a bunch of gunk on them that made his breath stink. And it made his mouth sore sometimes. The vet said cleaning his teeth would help."

Zach nodded, though he still didn't understand why a dog needed this service. He waited a minute, then spoke again.

"I bet you miss your buddy, though, huh?"

"Yeah, but Mom's going to get him when she gets off work."

The two sat in silence, eating their snack and gazing

into the fire. Zach noticed his young friend seemed distracted. He nudged Robert with his elbow.

"You okay, kid? You look kind of down."

Robert shook his head, then stopped and nodded. He shrugged and took another bite. Zach waited for him to speak up. It took a few minutes, but Robert finally spoke.

"I just found out my dad is alive."

Zach drew back in surprise. The kid had told him his father died when he was a baby. This had to be an enormous shock for the boy.

"Did your mom know?"

Robert nodded, his face miserable.

"Yeah. She's been lying to me all this time. I found the divorce decree in her important papers. He never even came to see me. They tried to explain it all to me, but it's still kind of hard to take, you know?"

Before Zach could respond to his young friend's statement, a rough voice interrupted.

"What's that kid doin' here?"

The two by the fire stood and turned toward the sound of the voice. Zach's stomach sank when he saw Mickey had returned while Robert was here. Now his friend would be sore at him for letting someone into their camp. Before he could say anything, Mickey tried to grab Robert. The boy blocked the move and stepped back with his hands raised for defense.

"Oh, we got us a little fighter here, huh? What, kid, you think you can take me on? How about if we bring a little something extra into it?"

Mickey pulled a gun out of his waistband and waved it around. Robert paled and took another step back.

Zach found the courage to speak up.

"Hey, Mick, you don't need that. This is my friend,

Robert. He was just leaving, right, Robert?"

He tried to catch the boy's eyes to send him a message to scram, but Robert's eyes focused on the pistol.

Mickey laughed, the grating sound sending shivers down Zach's spine. He wondered why he had never recognized before that his friend's laugh sounded evil.

"Don't worry, Zach, I won't hurt your little buddy. I only wanted to make a point."

He slid the gun into its holster, but stopped as he peered at Robert. His eyes widened, and a grin spread across his face. Mickey withdrew the pistol again and pointed it at Robert.

"Wait a minute. I thought I recognized you. You're the police chief's kid, aren't you? This is perfect. You've given me just what I needed."

Robert didn't answer or move. He stood as if frozen in place, his blue eyes wide and filled with fear. Mickey laughed again and waved his gun toward the door of the cabin.

"Let's go inside."

Zach's eyes darted between Mickey and Robert, a horrible sinking sensation growing in his stomach.

"Mick, wait! He's only a boy. He's my..."

"Yeah, yeah, I get it, he's your friend."

Mickey faced Zach, his dark eyes cold and hard.

"Aren't I your friend, Zach? Are you forgetting who protected you in prison when the gang wanted to beat you to a pulp? Who took you in when we got out?"

Zach wanted to protest that he was the one who opened his home to Mickey, but the words wouldn't come. He tried again to make himself stand up to Mickey, but could only stammer out a question.

"What..., what are you planning to do with him?"

"I'm going to hold him for ransom," Mickey growled. "I'll insist that the chief herself has to deliver it. When she arrives…"

Mickey grabbed Robert's arm in his meaty grip and jerked him toward the cabin, causing him to stumble on the rough ground and knocking the boy's red baseball cap into the dirt and leaves. When Robert tried to pull away, Mickey pointed the gun at the frightened boy's face.

"I said get inside! Zach, find that rope and tie the kid up. Do it right, you get me?"

Zach's stomach hurt and he thought he was going to be sick. This was his fault. He should never have allowed Robert to hang around the campsite. Now the boy and his mother were in danger. What could he do?

Robert shook in terror. What was this crazy guy talking about? He was holding him for ransom? His mom didn't make a lot of money. How was she going to pay any kind of ransom? Even if she did, it sounded like all this guy wanted was to hurt his mom.

He studied Mickey and tried to remember where he recognized him from, but at first the memory eluded him. Robert closed his eyes and concentrated. Then he remembered the rude guy that pushed him and Bear off the sidewalk the day they went to the nursing home. Now he realized that must have been Mickey. This man was more than rude - he was dangerous.

What could he do?

He stumbled again as Mickey prodded him into the house. Robert understood he needed to keep his cool, but right now he trembled like a scared little kid. The tears ran down his face as Zach tied him in the chair. He knew

Zach felt bad about this, but was afraid of the other man.

"Hand me that cell phone in his pocket. It'll have his mother's number in it. And make sure that rope is tight!"

Mickey's gruff voice sent chills through Robert's body. How did he know Zach had made the rope a little loose?

Robert's stomach cramped, and he thought he was going to be sick. God, are you there? I'm scared!

I am with you always.

A sense of calm came over him. God was with him, and he would choose to trust Him. He would trust his mom too, because he was sure she would do everything possible to get him back.

What if she came to get him and Mickey hurt her?

At the idea of Mickey hurting his mom, the terror rose again. He knew she would give her own life to save his. That was when Robert decided if he got out of this mess, he would give his mom a big hug and tell her he loved her and he forgave her.

Until that time, he would pray and watch for a chance to escape.

Chapter 12

Maggie took a cautious sip of the tea on her desk. She had been fighting a cough and sore throat all day and was pretty sure she had a fever. She laid her head on the desk for a moment as she fought a wave of dizziness.

"What's wrong, Maggie?"

She groaned when she heard the familiar voice. Maggie had hoped to hide her illness until she could get home and crash on the couch for the rest of the night. But Noah stood in her doorway with a concerned expression in his green eyes that even now drew her in.

"No!" she resisted those thoughts. Maggie could not, would not, give in to her attraction to her ex-husband. No way would she allow him to hurt her like that again.

Maggie raised her head and tried to act normal.

"Oh, I'm fine, just a little headache. It's been a busy day."

The sound of her own hoarse and weak voice belied her words. It irked Maggie to ask this man for anything, but she knew when she needed help.

"Noah, I think I've caught a cold. Can you do me a favor?"

"Sure! What do you need?"

Maggie didn't miss the eagerness in his voice. As bad as she felt, she knew she could not handle getting Bear from the vet. In fact, it would be a miracle for her to get herself home and in bed. She laid her head on the desk again and mustered the strength to speak.

"We had to take the dog to the vet for a teeth cleaning this morning. Can you pick him up and bring him to the house?"

"Of course, I'll be glad to get him for you. Is that all you need?"

Even with her eyes closed, Maggie sensed Noah's intense scrutiny. She forced herself to sit up so she could shut down her computer and put things away. When she stood and pushed her chair close to the desk, a violent coughing fit erupted. When it passed, Maggie wilted against her desk. It felt so good when Noah put his arm around her and helped her back into her chair.

"Why don't you let me drive you home first? Or do you want to go to your doctor?"

Maggie shook her head, then wished she hadn't when it protested by pounding in her temples.

"I think I just need to go home, but the ride sounds good. It's not a good idea for me to drive in this condition."

As Police Chief, Maggie tried to present a capable image. But right now, she felt about as strong as a piece of wet paper. It was inconceivable that she was letting her ex-husband take her home and get her dog for her. Maggie didn't want to depend on him for anything, but her illness held sway at the moment and she yielded to necessity.

Maggie followed Noah to his car, her legs shaking with the effort. When he opened the door for her, she sank into the seat with a sigh of relief.

After a quick stop at the vet's to pick up Bear, Noah drove to Maggie's home. When they pulled into her driveway, it surprised her to see the house was still dark. Robert normally had the lights on in the front room. A tendril of fear tickled the back of her mind. Where was her son?

Noah turned to Maggie.

"Isn't it unusual for the lights to be off? Robert's usually home by now, isn't he?"

Maggie slammed the car door open and jumped out, almost tripping over her feet in her haste. She heard Noah calling to her to wait for him, but she focused on one thing-ensuring her son's safety.

"Robert? Robert?! Robert!!!"

As she searched the house in frantic haste, Maggie flipped on light switches, as if the boy was playing hide-and-seek in the dark. The empty house seemed to echo her desperate voice as she called out.

"Maggie? Did you find him?"

Noah entered the house, leading a groggy Rottweiler. Bear sniffed around the house, searching for Robert. After not finding him, the dog came and sat in front of Maggie with a puzzled expression on his furry face, as if asking where she had hidden his boy. The sadness in the big dog's expressive eyes added to the burden of fear she carried.

Maggie turned toward her ex-husband, noting the worried expression on his face. She realized she needed to calm down and start acting like a police chief instead of a frantic mother. Easier said than done, she thought.

"No, he's not here."

She strode to the end table, where she kept a pad and pen. After jotting a few items, she handed it to Noah.

"Can you go to those places and look for Robert there? He may have just lost track of time. I'll start calling his friends to check if any of them have seen him."

Noah studied her face for a moment, then nodded. He would do as she asked, although it was obvious he was still worried about her. Funny thing. Since noticing that her son was not home where he should be, Maggie hadn't even noticed how sick she was. She steeled herself. She refused to give in to the illness or the fear. All that mattered was finding Robert and getting him home.

After Noah left, Maggie picked up her cell phone, hoping to find a text or missed call from her son. When nothing showed, she swallowed the tears and dialed the number for his best friend.

"Hi Charlotte, this is Maggie. Is Robert there?"

"Hi Maggie! No, Robert isn't here. Mike's been home all day with the flu. Come to think of it, you don't sound too good either. Are you coming down with something?"

"It's just a cold. I'm fine. Listen, if you see Robert, please tell him to call me. It's past time for him to be home."

"I certainly will. You poor thing! You must be terribly worried."

"Thanks, Charlotte! I have to go now. Take care."

Maggie felt bad about being abrupt, but Charlotte liked to talk and would have kept her on the phone for another hour. Maggie needed to make more calls.

After several calls to others who had not seen her son, the worry grew into a large specter of fear. Where could he be?

Just as she entered another number, her phone rang. The display showed Robert's icon. Relieved, Maggie swiped the phone to answer, her hand shaking.

"Robert, where are you, son? You should already be home!"

A low snicker met her words. Then a gruff voice answered.

"Your boy ain't going to make it home today, Maggie Jones. He won't make it home any day unless you do just what I say. Get me?"

Maggie sank into a nearby chair, her body trembling.

"Wha ... What do you want?"

"I want $50,000 in tens and twenties," the gruff voice replied. "You get the money. I'll call you back tomorrow morning and tell you where to bring it. If you don't do as I say or if I see any cops, I'll kill your boy."

"How do I know you have him?"

Her voice shook as she choked out the words.

"Mom?"

Maggie almost erupted in tears.

"Son? Are you okay? Has he hurt you?"

There was a long silence, then the man's voice came back on the line.

"I haven't hurt him yet, but I will. You get that money and be ready to bring it to me. Remember what I said-no cops. If I even *think* I see a cop, the boy dies. And I won't be using this phone when I call back, so you better answer whenever it rings, no matter what the number is."

Maggie went to her computer to track Robert's phone. As she opened the program, a sinister laugh sounded in her ear.

"Oh, and if you get any ideas about tracking him with his phone, just listen to this."

A slap echoed in the background, and her son cried out in pain. She winced as the noise of cracking plastic came through and the call dropped.

She punched in Robert's number, but it went straight to voice mail.

"Maggie? I tried those places you told me about, but he wasn't there."

Maggie turned toward Noah's voice. She tried to tell him about the phone call, but her throat refused to form the words.

"Mags? What's wrong?"

Darkness took her as she slid to the ground.

Noah almost missed catching Maggie. He knelt beside her and stroked her cheek. Her skin was hot and dry. Noah shook his head. Maggie should have been in bed, resting and taking care of herself instead of having to rush around to find Robert. Worry for mother and child filled his mind.

"Noah?"

Maggie's voice sounded weak and hoarse. He sat on the floor and pulled her to a sitting position, leaning her against his side.

"What's wrong, honey?"

The endearment slipped out before he could stop it. Noah hoped Maggie wouldn't pull away from him, but it seemed she didn't even hear him.

"A man called and said he has Robert. He demanded $50,000, and he wants me to deliver it. He said if he saw any police, he'd... Noah, he slapped my son. I heard Robert cry out in pain. What if he hurts him again? What if ...?"

Noah sighed when she said "my son" instead of our son and wondered if she would allow him to be a part of Robert's life when they got him back. He refused to even consider not getting him back.

"It's okay, Maggie. We'll get the money and get our son back."

Maggie struggled to get to her feet so that she could stand and face her ex-husband. She looked as if she would pass out again at any moment, but she stayed on her feet. She wore a fierce expression as she growled the words.

"No! He's *my* responsibility! I have to get the money

and meet the kidnapper tomorrow."

Noah surged to his feet. His temper rose as he realized she didn't even want to give him a chance to help rescue Robert. His son. This was ridiculous. *She* was being ridiculous! He opened his mouth to - what? He had no right to demand anything. If he tried, she might shut him out. He had to work with her, negotiate with her.

"Maggie, you're sick. You can hardly even stand up."

She stepped right in front of him and glared into his eyes.

"How do I know you aren't part of this? How do I know you and your friend didn't cook this up to take Robert away from me because I wouldn't let you…"

Maggie's shoulders slumped for a moment as she looked down, struggling with tears.

"Get out."

Noah stepped back as if she'd slapped him. He watched her swaying on her feet and prayed for wisdom. Then he stepped right into her space and captured her gaze with his.

"No," he told her in a firm voice.

"You will not shut me out at this critical time. Our son is in danger and I can help you get him back."

He took her by the shoulders in a gentle hold, relieved that rather than pull away or fight him, she just stared at him with wide, tear-drenched eyes.

"Maggie, I know I still have to prove myself. I didn't take Robert. I wouldn't do that to you. My friend Cy didn't take him either. He's a godly man who would never do anything to hurt anyone."

He looked away as a thought struck him. Cy! He still had contacts on the street. Cy might have the resources to rescue Robert. Noah turned back to Maggie and lifted her chin so that their eyes met.

"Listen to me, Maggie. I'm going to get our son back, okay? Then we can talk about what part you will allow me to have in his life, and in yours. Please don't push me away."

Maggie held his gaze for a long moment, then nodded. She realized she was in no shape to carry this off. Robert's life was more important than her pride or her hurt from the past.

"I guess I need to trust you right now," she breathed. "Please, don't let me down."

Noah brushed the hair out of her face.

"I won't," he promised. "I'll get him back, somehow."

Maggie woke from a troubled sleep. Noah had insisted she lay down and rest while he talked with his friend, but she didn't want to go to bed. They compromised on her stretching out on the couch. Laying down and pulling the afghan over her chilled, feverish body provided a sense of comfort that lulled her into slumber. Now she struggled to sit up so she could get back into the plan to find and rescue Robert.

Noah's friend, Cy, looked strange sitting at her dining room table, his shaved head reflecting the light. She still felt uneasy about pulling him into the situation. She didn't know this man, but she remembered arresting him years earlier. Noah tried to alleviate her apprehension by affirming that though Cy had been into drugs, both using and selling, he had accepted Christ while in prison and done a complete turnaround. Now Cy helped other men who struggled with the trap of drugs and alcohol; men like Noah.

The men's voices carried to the living room, though they talked in low tones; no doubt trying not to disturb her.

She leaned her head against the couch and tried to focus. Her throat was raw, and her head still pounded like a bass drum. From deep in her chest, a cough worked its way up. She tried to fight it, but the cough burst from her, anyway.

When she could breathe again without coughing, she looked up to see Noah bringing her a mug of hot tea. A smile curved her lips. When they first married, Noah believed a cup of tea with honey would cure anything. Her smile faded as she remembered the substances he substituted for tea later in their marriage.

She noticed Noah's puzzled gaze as he took in the change in her expression. Maggie didn't want to tell him about the memories that flashed through her mind. Instead, she reached for the mug and took a cautious sip. The warm, fragrant liquid soothed as it slid down her throat.

"Thank you," she whispered. It had been a long time since someone had taken care of her. Although most of the time she was a strong, independent woman, today she felt weak and vulnerable. Maggie figured it was probably whatever bug she had caught that was knocking her out, and she hated it. Her son needed her, and she could barely stand or talk.

"What's the plan?"

Maggie wanted to be a part of whatever they were planning. She needed to get the money together for the ransom and have it ready. In her head, Maggie understood giving the kidnapper money was not a good idea. But in her heart, where she fiercely loved her son, she would do anything to get him back.

Remembering the slap that echoed over the phone and the sound of Robert's voice crying out, Maggie visualized what she would do to the kidnapper if she ever got her hands on him. The plans that went through her mind for the thug were not pretty.

"Vengeance is mine, says the Lord," she tried to remind herself. But she didn't want to leave it to the Lord. She wanted to hurt the man who slapped Robert and took him hostage.

"Lord, I can't do this on my own," she whispered. "I need Your help."

She looked up into Noah's puzzled expression.

"Just asking for some divine help.

She patted the sofa next to her for him to sit down, then changed her mind and pointed to the chair angled nearby.

"I don't want you to catch whatever this is, but I need you to fill me in on what we're doing."

Noah and Cy settled in nearby chairs and the big man nodded at Noah to do the talking.

"Cy is going to do some checking around. He has a way of snooping things out."

As an amused glance of understanding passed between the men, the comradeship she witnessed touched Maggie. Noah had never had a wholesome, solid friendship with a male figure before. His "friends" during their marriage had been the ones who got him started drinking and using drugs. If Cy was the Christian man Noah said he was, then Maggie was glad to see that he had a friend like him.

"What will I do during that time?"

"Other than resting as much as possible, you're going to get the money ready and keep your phone handy for when he calls back. Do you have a way to trace the call if it comes on your phone?"

Maggie shook her head with a sense of defeat. She had wanted to get that technology, but their small town's budget would not allow it. The town council did not believe Forrestville experienced enough crime to warrant that kind of expenditure. Now she wished she had pushed harder for it.

Cy reached to touch Maggie's arm. She looked up into his serious dark brown eyes and experienced a flash of surprise at the compassion reflected there.

"Maggie, I will do everything in my power to find your son and get him back to you."

"Why?"

Instead of pulling away or reacting in anger, Cy gave her an understanding smile.

"You want to know why the guy you arrested for selling drugs is now helping you?"

Maggie nodded, her eyes intent on his face.

"When you arrested me all those years ago in Shreveport, I was a rotten sinner. I sold drugs, pimped, and even got into vicious fights where I inflicted terrible injuries. One man almost died because of me. But while I was in prison, someone told me about Jesus. He showed me how rotten I was and how good God is. By God's grace, He saved me from that life. Now I want to spend the rest of my life living for Him. Part of that is helping people in His name."

Cy stood and turned to face her.

"So, Maggie Jones, I am reaching out to help you because of His mercy and grace."

Maggie's eyes widened in amazement. That was the most talking she had heard from Cy since he came into the house, and she believed he meant every word. She closed her eyes for a moment to let it sink in, then opened them to gaze at the big man.

"Thank you," she whispered.

"You're welcome. Now, get as much rest as you can," he told her. "We'll see how this plays out."

He turned to Noah.

"I'm going to check out the town and see what I can

find out. I'll call you in about 30 minutes to give you an update. If the kidnapper calls, text or call me."

With that, the big man whirled away and left Maggie alone with Noah.

The room seemed empty without Cy's vibrant presence. Somehow, the man Maggie had despised now seemed like a friend. She leaned her head against the back of the couch and tried to stifle another cough.

When she thought she could talk again, Maggie opened her eyes. Resting seemed impossible right now, even as sick as she felt. She wanted to get up and search for Robert herself, but recognized she didn't have the strength. Maggie groped in her mind for something to distract her. She slanted her eyes toward Noah.

"He's a pretty impressive guy, isn't he?"

Noah nodded and grinned.

"Yeah, he's amazing. I don't think I've ever had a friend like him. He's more like a brother to me."

"How did you meet him?"

"Well, we had a nodding acquaintance for a few years while we both messed around with drugs. I used them, but Cy also sold them. Then I lost track of him for a while. We actually met up again when I was in jail."

Chapter 13

Noah tried to not notice the odor of stale sweat and urine that permeated the small cell as he flopped onto the thin mattress covering the metal shelf that passed as a bed. He didn't even want to think about who else might have slept on the mattress or what they might have left on it. Even the scent of disinfectant clinging to the material did not reassure him.

He sighed as he took in his accommodations for the night. He knew the drill. Picked up for possession, he would spend the night in jail and see the judge in the morning. What he didn't know was what would happen. Would this arrest be the one that got him more than a slap on the wrist?

A commotion sounded down the hall from him as raucous voices called out to someone passing by the cells. Noah heard what sounded like "Ty" or "Sigh." A few profanities rang out, followed by calls to "shut up!" He shook his head and rolled over, facing the wall. Someone had drawn some kind of a sick cartoon on the wall, so he turned back to face the door of the cell in time to see who the visitor was.

An imposing, dark-skinned figure paused outside the cell door and peered in at him. Noah thought he recognized the man as Cy Wilkerson, also known as "Brute" because of his size and meanness. Brute enjoyed a reputation as a *slick operator who knew how to sell- whether it was drugs, women, or other "services." No one messed with the man because they remembered what happened to the few who tried. But Cy was arrested and had dropped off the radar a few years prior.*

"Noah Jameson? Is that you, man?"

Something about the voice sounded different. There was a quality of - what? Light, that was it! Brute's voice had always carried a dark, menacing tone. Now the voice had a happy lift to it. Noah sat up and stared at his visitor.

"Don't you recognize me? I realize we only met a few times, but I figured you'd recognize me."

"Yeah, I recognize you. You just seem... different somehow."

Brute laughed and motioned for Noah to come closer.

"Come here and let me tell you about it."

"Watch out, Noah! You're dealing with a religious nut now! He even changed his name to Cy 'cause he's too good to be called Brute."

"Yeah, don't let him get to you!"

Noah had started toward the door until he heard the word "religious." Then he dropped back onto the bed, shaking his head.

"I want nothing to do with religion. My wife turned religious, and that made her leave me."

"Well, it's a good thing I'm not offering religion. I would like to talk to you about a Friend I have who made all the difference for me."

Noah stood and moved toward the door, curious about a friend who could change someone like Cy. The big man gave him a beaming grin that coaxed a small smile from Noah's lips. He couldn't help liking this guy.

"Who is your friend?"

"Jesus."

Noah wanted to turn away again, remembering Maggie's newfound faith in Jesus shortly before she left him. But the dark void in his life kept him standing and listening as Cy shared how Jesus found him and saved him, then changed him into the joyous man standing in front of Noah.

Tears ran down Noah's face as he realized how much he wanted what Cy had. But he didn't think God would take him. He had his chance when Maggie tried to talk to him and he rejected her- and her God.

"God won't want me. After Maggie found Jesus, she left me."

"Did Maggie leave you because she found Jesus, or because of the drugs and booze?"

Ouch! This guy knew how to get right to the point. Noah hated to admit it, even to himself, but Cy was right. Maggie's relationship with Christ had only made her sweeter and kinder. Noah recognized there was one person responsible for driving Maggie away. He looked at that man in the mirror every morning.

The realization drove a sharp pain through his heart and Noah crumpled to the floor, weeping. How could he have been so blind and stupid? Drugs and alcohol only made him sick and ruined. Maggie had been his reason for living until he let his addictions take hold.

Cy knelt on the other side of the door and watched Noah, compassion shining from his dark eyes. When Noah finished sobbing, he took a deep, shuddering breath, and raised his head to meet Cy's gaze.

"I want to know Jesus as my Friend too."

The smile Cy gave him was almost blinding.

"You can, brother. Do you also want to ask Him to be your Savior and Lord? You need to do that to know Him

as your friend."

Noah nodded. He bowed his head and repeated the prayer Cy led him through, then added his own words.

"Thank You, God. I'm sorry it took me so long. I will always regret the things I've done before meeting You."

Cy started to say something, then stopped and opened his Bible instead.

"Read this verse right here, Noah."

Noah focused on the small, clear print on the page Cy pointed out to him.

"If we confess our sins, He is faithful and just to forgive us our sins, and to cleanse us from all unrighteousness."

"Do you understand what that means?"

Noah stood, thinking. A slow smile crept onto his face. "It means I'm forgiven?"

"Exactly! God forgives you and makes you clean!"

Noah laughed with joy.

"I'm forgiven and clean!"

Maggie watched with awe as Noah recounted his story. The joy on his face and the peace in his eyes added extra weight to his words.

She realized she had been unfair to Noah ever since he arrived in her town. She had not even given him a chance to prove himself, but had held on to her anger and suspicions, even when he had shown himself to be honorable. Shame caused color to flood her cheeks. She turned her head to look out the window so Noah would not see the tears threatening to fall.

Maggie cleared her throat when she felt able to face him without crying, wincing when the action lanced her throat with pain.

"What happened after that?"

Noah sat in silence for so long, Maggie wondered if he had heard her question. She considered repeating it, but he spoke before she could get the words out again.

"I went to court the next day."

Noah slumped in his chair in the courtroom. The peace he had experienced the night before was now mixed with physical misery as his head pounded and his skin crawled. He realized he was going through withdrawal, but tried to control the tremors that shook his body.

The court-appointed lawyer glanced at him with pity and disgust. The older man had represented Noah in the past and made no secret of the fact he considered his client to be a bum. If he wasn't planning to plead guilty, Noah thought, he would ask for a different attorney.

"All rise."

Noah leveraged himself out of the hard chair and tried to stand up straight. Nausea swirled in his gut, but he clenched his teeth and resisted the urge to place his hand over his mouth or his stomach. When the judge pounded the gavel and announced the court was in session, the sound of wood on wood sent a shaft of pain through Noah's head.

"Mr. Jameson, I can't say I'm surprised to see you again, though I had hoped otherwise. You are entering a plea of 'guilty,' correct?"

Noah nodded, then spoke up.

"Yes, your honor. I want to face up to what I have done."

The judge stared at Noah, his face impassive. Noah couldn't tell if the judge was pleased, disgusted, or what. Just as the man opened his mouth to speak, a voice came from the back of the courtroom.

"Your honor, may I address the court?"

Noah turned and beheld Cy striding down the aisle wearing a suit and tie. Though he remembered Cy planned to be with him today, he still experienced a surprised sense of relief to see his new friend. Cy stopped by the table where Noah and his attorney sat and gave Noah a wink. Then he faced the judge and put on a serious expression.

"Mr. Wilkinson, it is good to see you again. I assume you are here to speak for the defendant?"

"Yes, your honor. I believe Mr. Jameson would benefit more from Christ First Rehab than from spending time in jail. You are familiar with the program and that we hold all of our students accountable. If the court will place Mr. Jameson in my custody and sentence him to attending the full program, I believe we can help him become a sober and productive citizen."

The judge allowed a small smile at Cy's description of the men in his program as 'students,' then turned a stern expression toward Noah, who waited for the punishment he understood he deserved. He didn't believe the judge would send him to Christ First Rehab. That's why his jaw dropped when the judge addressed Cy.

"Very well, Mr. Wilkinson. I will give you a chance to see what you can do with this sorry wreck of a man. Noah Jameson, this court sentences you to three years in jail for possession of cocaine and public drunkenness. Sentence is suspended as long as you follow through with Mr. Wilkinson's rehab program."

Noah sagged with relief and amazement, then looked up at the judge to thank him. The words died on his lips as his honor continued.

*"However, if you leave the program before completion or if you cause any trouble, I will personally make sure that you serve **every single day** of your sentence. Do I make*

myself clear, Mr. Jameson?"

Noah nodded, his throat tight with joy and trepidation. What if he failed? What if he couldn't finish the program? He realized the judge was waiting for a verbal response.

"Yes, Your Honor, I understand. I will do my best, sir."

A tiny glimmer of compassion showed on the judge's face.

"That's all I can ask of you."

Noah stood and paced around the living room, his eyes seeming to gaze into the past. Bear stood and watched, his back end slowly wagging. When he saw that Noah wasn't going anywhere, the dog lay down and rested his big head on the floor. Maggie took a sip of her tea and grimaced when she realized it had become cold. When Noah sat next to her again, she leaned forward, eager to hear more.

"So, how did you get to where you are now?"

Noah smiled as he leaned back.

"Cy is an amazing sponsor, but I had a tough time. Coming off of drugs and alcohol was a horrible experience. Though I knew God forgave me and gave me His peace and grace, the physical and mental cravings were terrible. But Cy and the other guys stayed with me and encouraged me all along the way. They didn't allow for any excuses, either. All of them had been through similar experiences and understood what I was going through."

Noah stood up and reached for her cup.

"Let me get you a fresh cup of tea and I'll tell you more, okay?"

Maggie waited, her pulse thrumming with anticipation. What Noah described to her was something she had prayed so hard for during those last two years of their marriage. Her throat tightened with repressed emotions as she fought to control the tears that insisted on stinging in her eyes. She didn't want to experiencel the compassion and warmth that welled up within her. Maggie kept telling herself it was too little too late, but realized that wasn't true.

Noah returned with a steaming cup of tea and another cup of chicken broth, which he arranged on the tray beside Maggie. She thought about protesting she wasn't hungry, but the tempting aroma from the broth teased her nostrils and made her mouth water. The broth would feel good on her throat, she reasoned.

As she took a tentative sip, she gazed at her ex-husband, waiting for him to get back to his story.

He laughed when he saw her face, and Maggie blushed at her transparency. Normally she maintained a reserved expression, but Noah's story had drawn her in. Finally, she couldn't stand the wait any longer.

"Please finish your story."

"Well, the rest is pretty anticlimactic as far as stories go. I graduated from the program and stayed on to help other guys like me. Cy let me live with him while I went back to school to finish my MBA."

Maggie remembered the arguments between them when Noah abandoned his higher schooling for the drugs and partying. She couldn't help a swell of gladness that he completed his degree.

"Cy helped me find a job with Sinclair Accounting Services, and I've been with them for a couple of years. I also got my CPA license. Lately I've been considering starting my own business."

He sat in thoughtful silence for a moment, then turned to look Maggie full in the face, his voice thick with emotion.

"Maggie, I know God has forgiven me and I hope you will as well. However, I will always regret our destroyed marriage and the time lost from knowing our son."

A tear ran down Noah's cheek and Maggie reached to wipe it away. Her heart hurt at the pain that now showed in his face. She laid her hand on his cheek for a moment, then moved to take another sip of the chicken broth. Maggie found herself with the crazy idea of taking Noah in her arms to comfort him.

When she thought she was past the wild notion, she spoke again.

"Noah, I can see I misjudged you and Cy. I'm glad God has given you such a godly man to be your friend. He's a remarkable man."

She took a sip of tea, then looked back at him.

"I think you're remarkable too.

Chapter 14

"Zach, get over here and leave the boy alone!" The younger man shot a frightened glance at Mickey. He reached out a trembling hand to pat Robert's shoulder. "It will be okay," he whispered. Zach didn't believe his own words, but he wanted to comfort his young friend.

"**Zach!**"

Mickey was roaring now, so Zach stood and almost tripped over his feet, trying to rush to stand in front of Mickey.

"I want you to go into town and get these supplies. Don't dawdle and don't talk to anyone. Get the stuff and get back here."

Zach took the list and the fistful of dollars that his friend handed him. As he stuffed them in his pocket, he gave Mickey a quizzical look.

"You don't let me go into town."

Mickey glared at him.

"I don't trust you not to let the boy go," he growled. "I'll stay here with the kid while you get the stuff. Remember what I said–no dawdling and no gabbing! Now git!"

Zach hurried to the door, casting a last glance over his shoulder at Robert. The boy's eyes were wide and red with recent tears. He hated to leave Robert alone with Mickey, but Zach felt he had to follow Mickey's orders. As he closed the door behind him, he heard Mickey snarling at Robert to "stop sniveling!"

Though he supposed he was taking a shortcut, Zach wound up going the long way to the small town. He hurried into the grocery store and gathered the items on the list. As he left, he heard footsteps approaching him from behind. Resisting the almost unbearable urge to check, Zach picked up his pace. He was almost to the corner when a gigantic hand came down on his shoulder. A deep voice called out to him.

"Hey, man, what's your hurry?"

Cy strolled down the sidewalks of Forrestville. Though able to enjoy its picturesque beauty as he walked, Cy was on the alert for anything that could help get Maggie's son home to her. At her insistence, they had not told the rest of the police force about the kidnapping. As far as Cy knew, no one else was aware that Maggie's young son was being held for ransom.

The whole thing seemed wrong, somehow. Why only $50,000? Cy suspected the kidnapper had something else in mind, like trying to lure Maggie into a trap. He understood a good cop like Maggie would have made enemies, and it was likely someone was trying to get even with her.

He glanced across the street and saw a man that looked familiar hurrying out of the small grocery store. A closer view confirmed Cy's suspicion. Yeah! He recognized that man. Zach had gone to prison for a short time for theft. While he was there, he had taken up with a bad dude–what was his name? Mickey, something. Cy always thought Zach could have straightened up and made something of his life if he had not gotten involved with Mickey.

Cy crossed the street and shadowed Zach. He knew Zach realized he was behind him when the smaller man's steps quickened. Cy lengthened his stride and caught up with him.

When Zach turned to face him, the fear in Zach's eyes startled Cy. He often forgot how large and imposing he seemed to others.

"What's up, Zach? Don't worry, I won't hurt you."

Zach gave a nervous laugh.

"Oh, is that you, Cy? I thought someone was going to mug me or something."

Cy glanced around, then back at Zach.

"In broad daylight? In this little town? You gotta be kidding! What are you doing here, anyway? Last I heard, you lived in Shreveport."

Zach trembled so hard he almost dropped his bag of groceries. Cy discerned there was something more happening. He gentled his voice.

"What's going on, Zach?"

"Oh, nothing. Me and Mi, I mean I'm doing some cold weather camping. That's all. Nothing else. Really."

Cy tried a different tack.

"So, you still hanging out with Mickey? Zach, I always thought you could make something of yourself if you'd quit hanging around him. You realize he's a destructive influence on you."

At that, Zach lost it. He started crying and blubbering something about a boy, a dog, a cabin in the woods, and that he didn't know Mickey was going to do it.

Cy's heart rate picked up. He took the groceries from Zach and led him to a nearby bench. Cy settled the bag of food on the ground and sat Zach on the bench. He lowered himself to a seat beside the weeping man and spoke in a firm but reassuring voice.

"Easy, Zach. Take a deep breath and tell it to me again slowly."

Zach gave him a suspicious look. Cy feared he was regretting spilling his story. He had to keep him talking.

"Please, Zach. This could be life or death for the kid and his mother. Tell me your story again."

Zach looked down at his hands that were clenched tight in his lap. Finally, he sniffled and nodded his head, as if coming to a decision.

"I met this kid, Robert, when he was hiking in the woods. He had a dog with him. One of those big kinds, black and brown, looks like a bear."

Cy fought a smile at the description. It was true, the Rottweiler did look like a bear. He nodded to encourage Zach to continue.

"Anyway, me and the kid get to be friends, you know? He stops by the cabin and talks to me, roasts hot dogs, stuff like that. Then Mickey comes up yesterday while the kid is still there. He recognizes Robert as the police chief's kid and tells me to tie him up. Afterward, he calls the police chief and tells her he wants $50,000."

Zach stared up at Cy, fear widening his eyes and roughening his voice.

"Mickey doesn't plan to let the kid go, though. He said he doesn't even care about the money. All he wants is to kill Maggie Jones 'cause he blames her for everything bad that has happened to him since she arrested him on a drug rap."

Cy sat in silence for a moment and considered Zach's story. Now everything made sense. His theory about the ransom money being a lure into a trap was right. He glanced back at Zach, who sat fidgeting and watching down the street.

When Zach moved to get up, Cy put out a hand to stop him.

"Where are you going?"

"Mickey told me to get the stuff and get back quick."

Cy shook his head. Zach was not a bad guy, but the wrong person could easily lead him down a ruinous path. The fact he hung out with Mickey proved that. Cy hoped to lead him to the Lord and away from the destructive lifestyle Mickey represented. But first, they needed to rescue Robert. He fixed his eyes on the smaller man.

"Zach, why do you hang around with Mickey? Why do you let him lead you into trouble like this?"

Zach stared at the ground while he mumbled something.

"What?"

"I said no one else will be my friend. They all see me as a loser."

Cy's heart ached for this man who only wanted to belong and to have real friends. He laid a hand on Zach's shoulder.

"You're not a loser, man. And I'll be your friend. But you can't go back and help Mickey with his plan. You'll be an accomplice to murder if you do."

An idea popped into Cy's head. He understood Zach hated being a part of Mickey's plan to kill Robert and Maggie. If given a way out, he believed the younger man would take it. Cy shot a quick glance around, then took hold of Zach's arm and started walking toward Maggie's house.

"Where are we going?"

Zach tried to pull away.

"I have an idea that will save Robert and Maggie Jones, and keep you out of jail."

"Are you sure you know what you're doing?"

Noah's expression was dubious as he handed Cy the leash. Bear, however, couldn't wait to go. He pranced in a circle, licking any hands he could reach. Cy reached to rub the dog's head while he considered his friend's words.

"Well, I have part of an idea. I'm relying on the Lord's leading for the rest."

Noah's dubious expression changed to one of alarm. "Cy..."

"I know, brother, I know. There are two lives at stake here. But I believe God will provide a way through this. Let me introduce you to someone."

He motioned with his hand, and Zach stepped up, his face both hopeful and fearful. Cy understood the man was terrified of Mickey, but believed no one else wanted him. Crossing the one man who had seemed to befriend him had to feel like betrayal, yet he had agreed to help to save a child's life.

"Noah, did you ever meet Zach?"

"No, I don't think I have. What part do you play in this, Zach?"

Zach seemed poised to run, but at Cy's encouragement, he explained to Noah who he was and what he knew. Noah's expression grew thunderous as he listened. When it seemed as if he was going to unload on Zach, Cy intervened.

"My friend here is going to lure Mickey out of the cabin and away from the boy. I'll slip in and untie Robert and get him out."

"What is Bear going for?"

"To protect Robert if Mickey catches on. Zach here tells me that Bear and Mickey have met before. I don't think Mickey will want to tangle with a protective Rottweiler again."

Zach spoke up.

"Um, Mickey has a gun, and he doesn't mind using it. What if he shoots Bear?"

"We'll work that out as we go."

Now both Noah and Zach gave him doubtful looks. Cy saw their expressions and sighed.

"Look, guys, it's all we have. Come on, let's pray before Zach and I get started."

Though Zach tried to pull away, Cy pulled him forward as the men bowed their heads.

"Lord, we need Your guidance, protection, and strength," Cy prayed. "Please help us rescue this young man who is in danger. We pray for You to put a hedge around his mother and give her healing and comfort. Also, we ask You to help Zach make right choices now and find new friends who will appreciate him for the man he is and the man You will make him become. In Jesus' mighty name we pray, amen."

The group broke apart. While Zach turned his face to hide the tears in his eyes, Noah turned to Cy.

"What do you want me to do?"

"Go back to Maggie and tell her what we're doing. Mickey may call her soon for the ransom. Get her to keep him on the phone as long as possible. I want him distracted when we approach the camp."

"You understand she won't like being kept out of the loop."

"Let her know she's still in the loop. Her part is to talk to the kidnapper when he calls. She has to keep him on the phone and distract him for us. She can't walk into this camp. She's the one he wants and if she goes in there, he'll kill both her and Robert."

"I'll tell her. Then I'll sit on her to get her to stay put."

Both men laughed at the idea of Noah sitting on Maggie, but soon sobered and shook hands.

"I'll be praying," Noah promised.

"Pray hard!"

Cy watched Noah as he turned to go back to Maggie's home. Then he turned to Zach and waved him forward.

"Let's go. We have a boy to rescue."

Zach swallowed hard and attempted a smile.

As the trio approached the camp, Zach slowed, then held up his hand for Cy and Bear to stop. He took a firmer hold on the bag of groceries and looked at Cy.

"I'm going to call for him as I walk up. When he comes to the door to yell at me, I'll drop the bag and back up. You and the dog sneak around back. There's a window with a weak catch. You should be able to get in. Can you trust that dog to stay quiet and not start barking?"

"I think he'll behave. He seems to have some training. You try to keep Mickey out front as long as possible."

Zach stepped out and headed for the campfire. When he was clear of the woods, he called out.

"Mickey! Hey! I'm back!"

The cabin door flew open, and a hulking figure appeared with a cell phone to his ear. He waved an impatient hand, motioning for Zach to be quiet while he gave gruff orders on the phone. Zach stopped and watched, understanding that Mickey was talking to Robert's mother. He overheard him tell her to meet him at the edge of the woods near Main Street and to bring the money in a backpack. Zach hoped Cy's plan would work and Mickey would go to jail instead.

After Mickey ended the call, he glared at Zach.

"What took you so long? And why did you come

in here yelling like that? You idiot! Do you want some hunter to hear you and come check us out?"

Zach stepped back in fear as Mickey strode toward him.

"Give me that bag, you moron. Did you get everything I told you to get?"

"I, uh, I think so."

"You think so? Didn't you use the list? Geez! Do I have to do everything?"

When Mickey was a few steps away, Zach dropped the bag of groceries. He couldn't help cringing when Mickey towered over him.

"What did you do that for? You klutz! I wonder what I keep you around for. You're useless! You better not have broken anything or I'm going to break you!"

Cy heard Mickey end his call and start belittling Zach. His stomach churned at the sound of the gruff voice raking over his new friend. After they rescued Robert, Cy would take great pleasure in taking Mickey down. He looked down at the panting dog and grinned. He was sure Bear would be happy to help with that.

When Cy eased up to the window and peeked through, he saw a young boy sitting in a wooden chair with his hands bound behind him. Cy tapped on the glass, and the boy jerked, his eyes growing round at the sight of the big man. A smile lit up Robert's face when Bear reared up, his massive head blocking the weak sunlight coming through the small space.

Cy grabbed hold of the window and pushed it all the way up. He tried to climb through, but realized his bulk would not fit through the small opening. Bear, however, did not have that problem. He leaped into the room and trotted over to his master, nosing around Robert's hands and chewing on the rope for a few seconds. After a moment, Robert pulled his hands free and hurried to remove the gag.

He ran to the window and tried to get Bear to jump out. The dog stood fast, however, refusing to budge until Robert climbed through. Just as Cy helped Robert down, Mickey entered the cabin.

"Hey, you!"

He blistered the air with a string of profanity and moved to intercept his victim, but skidded to a stop when faced with an angry Rottweiler. Bear emitted a low growl in the thug's face as the hair around his hackles stood up, and his teeth showed in a vicious snarl. Mickey howled and jumped back, then scurried away to hide behind a large crate. He pulled a pistol from his waistband and peeked out to where the dog had stood. When he saw the empty place where the Rottweiler had stood, Mickey jumped from his shelter and lumbered to the door.

Cy and Bear ran with Robert around the cabin to meet up with Zach, who had moved to the edge of the woods to wait for them.

"Zach! I knew you wouldn't let him hurt me!"

Robert threw his arms around Zach. The young man gave the boy a quick hug, then turned him toward the woods.

"Hurry! He'll be out here any second now!"

As he spoke, the cabin door flew open and Mickey charged out, yelling threats and waving the pistol. When he stopped to take aim, Zach pushed Robert toward Cy.

"Go on, get out of here. I'll try to stop him."

Zach turned back to talk to Mickey, who only glared at him. Before he could get a word out, Mickey pulled the trigger, and a bullet whizzed past Zach.

"You traitor! After everything I've done for you, how could you turn against me and set this up? You worthless piece of…"

The gun sounded again, and Zach grabbed his shoulder and stumbled back, dropping to his knees, the blood seeping through his fingers.

Before Mickey could fire another shot, Bear launched himself at him, his powerful jaws clamping on his wrist and causing the shooter to drop the weapon. Mickey screamed in fear and pain as the Rottweiler growled and shook him, tossing him to the ground like a rag doll.

Cy helped Zach to his feet and pushed him toward the woods, where Robert wrapped a supporting arm around his waist and began leading him away. Once the pair were safely down the path, Cy sauntered to the kidnapper, who lay on the ground blubbering. The gun lay beside him, so Cy picked it up and unloaded it, putting both the bullets and the gun in his front pocket. He stood in silence, watching the crying man and the dog who held him fast.

Mickey turned a pleading look toward him, his eyes widening when he recognized the big man.

"Cy! Hey man, get this vicious animal off of me! He's trying to kill me!"

"Bear, release."

Cy spoke the command in a low tone, but the dog obeyed and stepped back, though he continued to growl and show his teeth.

Mickey raised to a sitting position, but eyed the big dog as if afraid he would attack again.

Cy grabbed hold of Mickey's shoulder, his grip just tight enough to cause pain.

"Get up, Mickey. You're coming with me to the police station."

The thug glared up at him.

"Why would I do that? Do you think I'm stupid?"

"Do you really want me to answer that? You're coming because I'm placing you under citizen's arrest for kidnapping and attempted murder."

Cy pulled Mickey to stand and marched him into the woods, where they could see Zach and Robert a couple hundred yards ahead. At Cy's command, Bear ran to join the two. Cy wanted the big dog with Robert and Zach for protection.

As the two men hiked along the path, Cy noticed Mickey's expression change from sullen to shifty. Just as he wondered what the man was plotting, Mickey turned and hit Cy on the head with a branch that he had picked up and hidden on his other side. The blow caught Cy near his left eye and scratched down the side of his face.

As Cy recoiled from the blow, Mickey twisted away from his grip and slipped away into the woods. Cy wiped away the blood and realized he did not know which way the man had gone. He could find his way around in the woods, but he knew nothing about tracking. As he hurried to catch up with Zach and Robert, Cy shook his head in disgust with himself.

"Man! I can't believe I fell for that trick! Now the creep has gotten away and Maggie and Robert will never be safe with him loose. We have to get Robert home, then find Mickey-and fast!"

Zach winced as he stumbled, jarring the wounded shoulder. He glanced back, expecting any minute to see Mickey charging through the woods, screaming and blaming Zach for everything that went wrong with his kidnapping plan. Just like he blamed Zach for everything else. Mickey never admitted to being wrong. It was always someone else's fault.

"Hey, aren't you Mr. Jameson's friend? I think I met you at the barbecue."

Zach startled at first when Robert spoke because he had been so deep in thought. He glanced at Cy and observed him smiling down at Robert.

"Yeah, we've been friends a long time."

The boy walked along without speaking for a moment, his strong young arm still supporting Zach. He said his next words in a low tone.

"He's my dad, you know. I found out a few days ago."

Zach peered down at his friend. This was the story Robert had started to tell him when Mickey interrupted. When he glanced at Cy, he saw understanding on his face.

"Yes, I know about that too."

They came to the edge of the woods and Cy tried to steer them toward the hospital. Zach pulled back in fear.

"I don't want to go to the hospital."

Cy and Robert gave him identical puzzled looks.

"Why not?"

"I, I'm afraid of hospitals."

Zach felt like a wimp, admitting even that much. Every time he had been to a hospital, he went to jail afterward. He understood he deserved jail, but he sure didn't want to go.

"Zach, you're bleeding. You need medical attention right now."

"No!"

He looked up with pleading in his eyes.

"Let's just take Robert home to his mother, okay? Maybe, maybe she can give me some first aid."

Cy stood and stared at him for a moment, then nodded and directed them toward his car, though he mumbled something about first aid not doing much good.

"Hey, Zach?"

Zach met Robert's eyes.

"Yeah?"

"Thanks."

Zach experienced a warmth inside that he had never known. Was this what genuine friendship was like? He squeezed the boy's shoulders.

"You're welcome."

Chapter 15

Maggie paced her living room, stopping every few steps to glare at Noah.

"I still don't see why you won't let me take the money and try to catch the man who took Robert. What if Cy and Bear can't get him? What if this man Zach double-crosses Cy? How do we know he wants to help?"

Maggie didn't realize she was crying until one of her tears fell on her hand. She swiped her hand across her eyes to wipe away the moisture, then collapsed onto the couch.

"Maggie, you're in no shape to take this man on. Honey, you can barely walk a few steps."

"You and your friends are interfering with a police matter! And don't call me honey!"

Noah captured her gaze with his own, his green eyes full of sympathy.

"If you'll recall, Maggie, you didn't even call the police. Right now, you are not Forrestville's police chief. You are a sick, worried mother who is frantic about her child's safety. Cy will bring him home."

Maggie leaned her head back and closed her eyes. She hoped Noah was right. He had informed her that Cy excelled at ferreting out information, but that was not the same as taking on a dangerous criminal or rescuing a kidnapped child.

Just as Maggie got to her feet to pace again, there was a commotion at the back door. The door banged open, and Bear bounded inside. Cy and a man bleeding in his shoulder came next. Last came the face Maggie feared she would never see again.

"Robert!"

Mother and son embraced, both weeping, smiling, and trying to talk. Robert pulled away and laid his hand on Maggie's forehead.

"Mom, you're sick! Your skin is so hot!"

Maggie smiled and laid her hand on his cheek.

"I'm fine now that you're home."

When she spotted the bleeding man, she stood and took charge.

"Robert, get a couple of towels and bring them to me. Cy, lay him on the couch and take a towel. Apply firm, steady pressure on the wound. Noah…"

Noah took her hands and pulled her toward the couch she had vacated.

"Sit down, Maggie. We'll take care of this."

Once the excitement died down, Cy and Robert took turns telling Noah and Maggie their story. When Robert described how Zach stepped in front of Mickey, Maggie turned toward Zach with tears. She had to push the words past the lump in her sore throat.

"Zach, I can't believe what you endured for my son. 'Thank you' is not enough, but I mean it with all my heart."

He gave her a weak smile and murmured, "You're welcome."

After the two finished their story, Maggie stood and walked to stand in front of Cy. She bent over and kissed him on the cheek.

"Cy, I can't thank you enough, either. I'm sorry I doubted you. Without your intervention, Mickey might have killed us both."

Cy blushed at the thanks, but a grim expression shadowed his face.

"I only wish I hadn't let him get away. I should have known he'd try something."

"Don't worry. I'll put out a BOLO on him. We'll catch him."

"But you and Robert won't be safe until he's caught."

Though still feverish and achy, Maggie felt as if she could take on anything or anyone now that her son was home with her. She stood tall in front of the group.

"Don't worry. I'm used to dealing with dangerous criminals. Now, let's get this man to the hospital. Robert, while we get ready to go, why don't you feed Bear. Give him a little something extra on his kibble. He deserves more than that, but we'll start with a jerky treat for now."

Robert sent a dazzling smile to his mother and ran to do what she said. Maggie turned around in time to catch a silent communication between Noah and Cy.

"What?"

Noah stepped next to Maggie and took her elbow as Cy helped Zach off of the couch.

"Well, since we have to take Zach to the hospital, how about if you get checked out, too?"

"I don't think that's necessary."

"Well, we do. You're still feverish and hoarse."

When Maggie opened her mouth to protest again, Zach spoke up, his voice shaking a bit with weakness.

"Chief Jones, I would sure feel better if you were at the hospital with me. Please come. They can check you out while they take care of me."

Maggie eyed Noah and Cy. She knew they were conspiring together, but she couldn't turn down the request of the man who got shot defending her son. She deflated.

"Oh, all right! I will let them check me out, too. Let's go."

Maggie sat beside Zach in the back seat of Cy's SUV and held a fresh towel on the wounded shoulder. She didn't want to disturb him, but a question had popped into her mind that would not go away. Finally, she had to ask.

"Zach, why does Mickey want to kill me?"

The injured man didn't answer at first, then with a quick peek at Maggie, he told her what Mickey had told him. His expression was half-defiant, half-fearful that she would punish him for Mickey's transgression.

Maggie felt compassion for this young man. He had been under the influence of a bitter, angry man who wanted to blame others for the consequences of his own evil actions. She hoped he would make something better of his life now that he was away from Mickey.

As she thought about how long Mickey had hated her, she experienced a jolt inside. Was she any better? She had held onto her hurt and anger toward Noah for almost thirteen years. When she and Robert had a tough time, she blamed Noah for not being there, for not being a good husband and father. Had she allowed bitterness to fester inside herself? What kind of witness had that shown?

Before she could think any more about it, Cy pulled the vehicle in at the Emergency Room at Forrestville General. He and Noah helped Zach out, while Robert took charge of getting his mother into the ER. When Maggie saw how seriously her son took his responsibility, she cooperated, even leaning on him a bit.

A nurse whisked Zach away for x-rays while another led Maggie to an exam area. An older lady in nurse's scrubs took Maggie's vitals and tsked when she saw her temperature.

"103 degrees. Chief Jones, you should have been in here a lot sooner. And listen to that cough! Now, you just lay back here and the doc will be in to see you in a jiffy."

The nurse fluffed Maggie's pillow and helped her get comfortable on the bed.

Maggie resisted, feeling the need to stay alert, but relaxed despite herself while she waited. Now that Robert was safe, it felt good to rest. She closed her eyes and the next thing she knew, her family doctor was standing over her. Maggie tried to sit up, but he held up his hand, motioning for her to lie down again. She settled back on the pillow and smiled into her doctor's face.

"Dr. Barry! What are you doing here?"

The doctor gave her a mischievous grin.

"I somehow knew my favorite patient needed me here." He laughed.

"I'm helping in the ER during the flu season. They've had a large influx of patients and needed some extra hands. Now, let me look at you."

After checking her over and asking a few questions, Dr. Barry ordered lab and x-rays. Maggie wanted to object, but realized it wouldn't do any good. Now that she was in the ER, they were going to check her out thoroughly.

After various stops for the tests, Maggie returned to the exam area. She laid her head back to rest and watched for Dr. Barry to come back with the results.

After what seemed like an interminable wait, the older man came through the curtain. He put the x-ray films on the light box and studied them for a moment. After a long moment, he flipped through her chart. He looked up when she asked what he saw.

"Maggie, you don't have the flu or strep throat."

"Oh, thank goodness! I can't afford the time off."

He fixed her with a stern glare and continued.

"You do, however, have a sinus infection and a severe case of bronchitis. It looks like you have a throat infection as well. I'm going to give you some antibiotics and some orders I expect you to follow, young lady."

Maggie had to smile at being called "young lady." She didn't feel young after the past twenty-four hours.

"I'm listening, doc."

"I want Robert to hear this too so he can make sure you follow orders."

Dr. Barry spoke a few words to the nurse. A few minutes later, Noah and Robert entered the room. Robert stood by his mother, taking her hand in his and giving it a squeeze. After hearing about his ordeal at Mickey's hands, the ER staff had examined him as well. Other than the bruise on his cheek, he seemed to be fine.

Maggie knew, however, that her son had been through a very traumatic experience. It would take time for his heart and mind to heal. In the meantime, she would make sure he stuck close to her.

"Are you listening, Maggie? I want you to go home and rest. No work, no housecleaning or cooking, REST! You got that?"

Robert spoke up.

"Sir, I will make sure she minds you."

Noah stepped to Maggie's side.

"I'll help make sure she follows orders."

The doctor gave him a curious glance. He didn't ask

who Noah was, but Maggie saw the question on his face. With a quick glance at Noah, Maggie answered.

"He's a close friend of the family."

Dr. Barry nodded and wrote out the prescription for Maggie, which he handed to her with a wink.

"Looks like you're well cared-for. Just make sure you mind what I say. We want you to get well as soon as possible."

Chapter 16

After filling her prescription, Noah and Cy brought Maggie and Robert home and then hovered over mother and son. Maggie had to laugh at them.

"You're like a couple of mother hens!"

Cy and Noah chuckled at the sight of each other with aprons swathed around their middles and towels thrown over their shoulders. Noah winked at Maggie, causing her to blush as he brought her another cup of hot tea.

After cooking dinner, cleaning up, and taking care of the animals, Noah and Cy had to admit they were tired and ready to return to their motel rooms for a good night's sleep. Maggie thanked them both and sent them on their way. Though thankful for the part each had played that day, she was ready for some quiet time with her son.

Because of the bronchitis, Maggie opted to spend the night in the recliner to help her breathe better. When Robert learned she was staying in the living room, he announced he would sleep on the couch.

"Oh no, young man. You need your rest. You've been through a hard couple of days."

"Mom, I'll rest better if I'm close to you. Please?"

Maggie saw the strain and anxiety on his face and relented. At this point in time, she didn't want to be very far away from him, either.

Robert made himself a comfortable nest on the couch with a pile of blankets and pillows, while Maggie settled into her recliner with a relieved sigh. They turned off all the lights except for a small lamp next to her chair. Bear settled on the floor next to Robert, and Cookie curled up in Maggie's lap.

Maggie had almost drifted to sleep when Robert's voice came to her.

"Mom, I want you to know, I forgive you for lying to me. And, I trust you again."

Maggie had to work to control her voice. She reached for a tissue and blew her nose, trying not to break down sobbing.

"Mom, are you okay?"

"I'm okay."

She paused.

"You don't know how much that means to me. I'm sorry I told you your father was dead, Robert. Even though I thought I had a good reason, it was wrong for me to lie to you. I will try very hard from now on to always be honest with you."

They both lay still for a moment, then Robert spoke again.

"I guess Jesus would want me to forgive the man that kidnapped me."

She struggled with that herself. As a Christian, Maggie knew she should forgive the man and pray for his salvation. As a mother whose child he had hurt and threatened, she wanted to tear Mickey into tiny pieces and grind those pieces into dust. She took a deep breath and shook the image from her mind.

"Yeah, I guess we both do. You know what the Bible

says about forgiving?"

"Yes, ma'am. But it's really hard. I'm not just mad at him for hurting me and Zach. He wanted to kill you and I'm still scared of him."

Maggie fingered the pistol at her waist. She had put the holster on under her pajamas and slid the Glock into place before leaving her room. That evil man would not get a chance to hurt her son again.

"I understand, son. It is hard to forgive him, knowing how evil he is."

Maggie realized this was a teaching moment. She was struggling to forgive a man she might have to shoot to protect her son. But, she had a responsibility to teach her son Biblical principles. She tried to mean what she was about to say.

"How about if we pray and ask God to help us forgive? Can you do that?"

Robert was quiet for so long Maggie thought he'd gone to sleep. After a long silence, a small voice answered.

"Yes, ma'am. I'll ask Jesus to help me be willing."

Maggie smiled in the darkness. Her son was growing into such a godly young man. Then his next question pierced her thoughts.

"Mom? Have you forgiven Mr. Jameson for hurting you when he was on drugs?"

Now it was Maggie's turn to be silent for a long time. She had been asking herself for several days if she could do that very thing. Somehow, now, it seemed more possible. Yet a part of her still feared being hurt again. Maggie didn't want to dwell on how Noah could hurt her now, though she recognized her growing attraction to her ex-husband made that possible. She realized Robert was waiting for an answer.

"Son, I'm praying about that."

Robert slid his hand toward where hers rested on the arm of the recliner. He grabbed her hand and squeezed for a minute before letting go.

"I'll pray too."

Mickey slumped behind the wheel of his car and stared out at the dark woods, his eyes smoldering with rage. He couldn't believe how everything had fallen apart, and all because his *supposed* friend had betrayed him. Betrayed him! To save that brat and his mother! Mickey slapped the steering wheel, then winced at the pain in his hand.

Well, he would fix them all. He would eliminate them, one by one, if he had to, including the big, bald dude. Mickey remembered when Cy was a drug dealer himself. Then he went and got religion while he was in prison. Well, Cy shouldn't have stuck his nose in where it didn't belong.

He felt a shiver of fear, thinking about the big Rottweiler that had leapt to the boy's defense. Yeah, that dog had to go too. It had interfered with his plans twice now. He would enjoy shooting the dog and listening to its cries of pain.

Mickey was glad he had hidden the car in a dark, secluded area of the woods, away from the camp. He knew the possibility of discovery existed and he wanted a way out of there if needed. But he wasn't leaving yet. He would kill Maggie Jones and everyone she cared about.

But what was the best way to do it? Mickey leaned the seat back and settled into the car's threadbare cushions as he considered his options. A plan developed in his twisted mind and he couldn't help grinning as he imagined each step of the way. He would find another hiding place for a while, then watch for the perfect opportunity.

He lay still for a moment, staring into the darkness that surrounded him. No matter how he squirmed, Mickey could not get comfortable. He sat up and adjusted the seat. No need to suffer in the car. He could find a more comfortable spot and set his plan in motion tonight.

Mickey drove to a small town near Shreveport and checked into a cheap motel. The night clerk welcomed him with a cheerful greeting, but Mickey only grunted as he accepted the room key.

He stayed in the motel room for a week, keeping a low profile and only venturing out to pick up food and beer. After the week was up, he stopped at a nearby dollar store to pick up a few supplies. When Mickey spotted a thrift store across the street, he ambled over to check it out. Thirty minutes later, he exited the store, bag in hand and a satisfied smirk on his grizzled face.

Back in the motel room, he showered and shaved, even putting on a splash of aftershave. He swore as it stung the minor cuts on his chin. After he cleaned up, Mickey stepped over to the bed and held up the clothes he had purchased.

When he had seen the minister's shirt and collar at the thrift shop, his plan just seemed sweeter. Mickey knew he couldn't go into the hospital looking like a bum or wearing the black clothes and the ski mask. That would set off security for sure.

But, as a preacher! Yeah, that was perfect. No one would suspect a thing if he went in wearing this stuff. With him wearing this getup, the hospital employees would probably show him where he needed to go. Then he could get to Zach's room and teach that traitor a lesson. The last lesson

Zach would ever learn.

Mickey pasted on a smile as he walked through the hospital doors. He clutched the Gideon Bible he had swiped from the motel room and looked around for the admitting desk. There! A pretty young lady in scrubs was talking on the phone while handing some forms to an older couple.

He walked up and waited his turn, trying to think how a preacher would look when he came to the hospital to call on sick people.

"May I help you, sir?"

Mickey assumed a genial air as he lowered his voice to speak to the clerk.

"Yes, my name is Reverend Stanfield. I'm here to visit one of my church members, Zach Turner. Can you tell me what room he's in?"

"Sure, let me look that up for you."

Mickey looked around him while the receptionist clicked the keys on her computer.

The hospital lobby was clean and bright, with pale blue walls and white curtains. A large fish tank took up part of a wall and several children clustered in front of it, pointing and exclaiming over the bright tropical fish that swam in the clear water.

Nearby a few small tables sat near the couches and chairs, with some old magazines and a couple of books spread out on them. Tantalizing aromas came from a coffee station set up in the corner and reminded Mickey he had skipped breakfast. He could sure use a cup of the hot brew right about now.

"Here you go, Reverend. Room 141, bed 2. Just go down this hallway and turn right. It's a few doors down on the left."

Mickey abandoned the idea of getting a cup of coffee

as he thanked the young lady, then strode toward Zach's room. He wanted to walk fast and get this done, but he forced himself to walk more slowly. It might not look right for a preacher to run to a hospital room.

On the way down the hall, Mickey had realized there might be someone else in the room. He would have to change his plan if Zach had a roommate. Maybe he could "invite" Zach to go for a walk with him. Only if Zach recognized him, he might yell for help instead. He'd have to take it slow until he could see if Zach was alone.

As he approached, Mickey also realized Zach might have police guarding him. His eyes darted around the hallway, searching for police officers or security guards. When he saw the door standing open partway with no one guarding, he released a pent-up breath. If he had had to take out a guard, that would have complicated things.

He found the room and entered without knocking. Glancing at the other bed, Mickey saw it was stripped and empty. Good. There would be no witnesses.

Zach looked up with a welcoming smile.

"Hi, Reverend! Are you looking for someone?"

Mickey approached the bed and laid the Bible on the nightstand.

"Yes, Zach. I'm looking for you."

Zach's face showed confusion, then recognition.

"Mi... Mickey! What are you doing here?"

Zach's hand groped the sheets as if searching for something. Mickey took great pleasure in watching the fear grow in his former friend's eyes. He picked up a pillow from the empty bed and moved toward the younger man.

Just as he had placed the pillow over Zach's face and applied pressure, the door to the room opened and a nurse walked in.

"Mr. Turner, the doctor will be in soon to discuss your discharge. But there's still time for break... What are you doing?!"

The nurse screamed and backed out of the room, calling for security. Mickey swore and threw the pillow across the room. He yanked the door open and bolted down the hallway, shoving aside anyone who got in his way.

A security guard hurried into the hall, pulling his gun from his belt.

"Stop or I'll shoot!"

Mickey disregarded the man. He knew the guard wouldn't shoot. There were too many people standing in the way.

He pushed through a fire exit and ran down the street, stopping when he reached the edge of the trees. Mickey leaned against a tree trunk to catch his breath.

So much for his plan! He had thought to kill Zach first, then the boy. Lastly, he would find Maggie Jones and take great pleasure in telling her what he'd done to her son. After watching her scream and cry about that, he would kill her. The dog and Cy would die later.

Well, he just had to make adjustments, that's all. He would forget about killing the others. They were just extras, anyway. His primary goal was to kill the police chief. Then he would take off and maybe go live in Mexico.

After the disaster at the hospital, Mickey knew he would need to move fast. He decided to drive back to Forrestville and find a good hiding place in town. He would watch for a chance to get Maggie alone.

Then it would all be over.

Chapter 17

Noah tried to tamp down his irritation as he parked in front of the police station. He had gone to Maggie's house to check on how she was feeling and invite her to lunch. When he got there and rang the doorbell, no one answered. A sense of alarm ran through him until he peeked in the garage window and noticed he did not see Maggie's small SUV. Now he was looking at it two spots down from his parking place.

He shook the water from his umbrella as he stepped into the station. After depositing it in the urn designed for wet umbrellas, Noah waved to Linda on his way to Maggie's office. The young woman was on the phone, so he just motioned he was going to see the police chief.

A soft "come in" greeted his knock on the office door. Noah stuck his head in the door and saw Maggie talking on the phone. She waved at him, so he stepped in and sat in the nearest chair, studying her while he waited.

Her blue eyes seemed to sparkle today and there was a slight flush to her cheeks. To Noah, Maggie was beautiful, and he wanted nothing more than to court her and win her back. But he didn't know if she would ever trust him with her heart again.

When she hung up and gave him an expectant look, it

took Noah a moment to realize she was waiting for him. He shook his head and tried to remember why he had come. After a moment, it came to him.

"Aren't you supposed to be at home resting?"

Noah realized too late how accusing he sounded. Before he could backtrack, Maggie laughed at him, her eyes twinkling in amusement.

"Stop being such a mother hen! I'm fine. I'm taking my meds and making sure I drink plenty of fluids."

Noah chuckled.

"You're right. I guess I am hovering."

He hesitated before adding.

"It's just because I care and I don't want you to get sick again."

Maggie blushed and looked down at her blotter, fidgeting with her letter opener. When she looked up at Noah, the soft expression on her face sent a thrill of amazement through him. Maggie stood and slid her pistol into her holster, then motioned to him.

"Let's take a walk. I need to talk to you about something."

Uh oh! This did not sound promising. What did she want to talk to him about? Was there a problem?

"What..."

He started to ask her, but she shook her head.

"Not here. I want a little more privacy."

"Maggie, it's pouring rain outside! And have you forgotten about Mickey? He's still out there and he still wants to kill you."

"I know about the rain and about Mickey. We have umbrellas, don't we? And my officers have searched this town and the woods for that thug. In all likelihood, he hightailed it back to Shreveport and is hiding there since his kidnapping plan failed. I sent a report to the Shreveport office of the FBI. They'll take it from here."

When Noah's face registered concern, Maggie stepped close to him and laid her hand on his arm.

"I'm not being careless, Noah. Of course, we'll keep an eye out for him. But I need to talk to you."

Noah drank in the sight of this beautiful woman who wanted to take a walk in the rain with him. He opened the door and waved her through. At the urn, he handed her the purple umbrella he knew was hers and reached for his. She laid her hand on his arm again.

"Mine is big enough for both of us."

Startled, he dropped his umbrella back into the stand.

"Are you sure?"

He couldn't believe she would even want to share an umbrella with him.

"I'm sure. Come on."

They walked in silence for a minute. When he tried to ask what she wanted to talk about, Maggie shook her head.

"Not yet. Let's get a little further from the station."

Though he tried to watch where they were going, Noah studied Maggie as they strolled down the wet sidewalk, their hands almost touching under the umbrella. She seemed nervous, but determined. He tried a little light conversation to break the tension until she was ready to tell him what she needed to say.

"Where's Robert?"

"He and Bear are at the dojo. I had to get special permission from Esther for Robert to have Bear in there. But when I told her about Mickey and the kidnapping, she said it was okay. Bear and Esther's German Shepherd, Ninja, seem to get along well, though I was a little nervous about that."

Silence fell between them again. Though apprehensive about what Maggie wanted to talk to him about, Noah enjoyed the sweet companionship they shared under the umbrella. Because of the rain, the streets were quiet, with little foot traffic.

"I think that's a great idea, having Robert keep Bear with him. I believe that dog would tear to pieces anyone who tried to harm his boy."

"That's the idea."

They came to a stop under the awning of a building that was up for sale. Noah glanced at a sign that read "Boyd's Accounting Services."

"What happened to the accounting firm?"

Maggie turned to discover what he was talking about.

"Oh, Mr. Boyd moved to New Mexico to retire. His daughter and her family live there and he wanted to be near them."

"Hmm. Is there another accounting firm in town?"

"No, most people go to Shreveport for anything more than basic bookkeeping."

Maggie coughed, and Noah laid his hand on her shoulder.

"Are you okay? Do you need to go back?"

She shook her head.

"No, I'm fine. I just, well, I need to tell you something, but I'm having a hard time finding the right words."

When she looked up at him, there were tears in her eyes. Noah worried he had hurt her somehow.

"Maggie, what's wrong?"

She tried to laugh, but it came out strangled.

"Noah, I guess the only way to do this is to come right out and say it. I forgive you."

Noah's heart stuttered. He had dreamed for a long

time about hearing those words from her. Now that he had heard them, the reality was even better than the dream.

"I forgive you and I want to ask your forgiveness."

"For what? I'm the one that hurt you."

"Yes, you hurt me. But I chose to hold on to the hurt and allowed bitterness to make me cold and hard toward you. That's not what Jesus would want me to do."

Maggie stopped for a minute, as if thinking about her next words.

"I want you to be a part of Robert's life. I can see the godly man you've become and I would be proud for you to be an influence for our son."

"Our son." Noah had never heard such sweet words, except for when Maggie said "I do." He tucked a loose strand of hair behind her ear as he gazed into her eyes, which the tears had turned into sparkling sapphires.

"What about you, Maggie? Can I be a part of your life?"

Before Maggie could respond, a sneering voice interrupted.

"Isn't that sweet? He wants to be a part of your life."

Maggie and Robert whirled toward the voice, realizing their mistake. They had been so absorbed in each other they had not watched around them. Stepping out of the nearby alley, Mickey waved a gun at them, a satisfied smirk spreading across his face.

"Too bad both of your lives are about to end."

"Linda, do you know where we can reach Maggie?"

The receptionist looked up from her computer, her eyes widening with concern at the serious tone of the officer's voice.

"She stepped out for a quick break. What's wrong?"

He huffed out an exasperated breath.

"That guy, Mickey, that kidnapped her son, showed up at the hospital and tried to kill Zach Turner."

"What? Oh no!"

"We need to get to Maggie before he does."

Maggie's officers had been furious with her when they learned she had concealed the kidnapping and allowed civilians to rescue Robert. Even after she explained Mickey had threatened to kill Robert if he saw any police, they still believed she should have included them. Now the kidnapper was at large and a definite threat to their chief and her son.

Linda tried calling Maggie's cell phone, but heard it ringing in the back of the station. She jumped up from her desk and hurried down the hall to Maggie's office. There on the desk sat the police chief's phone, plugged into a charger.

The receptionist strode back to her desk and tried the radio, but got only static. She turned worried eyes to the officer in front of her.

"Maggie's radio isn't working. What can we do now? There's no way to reach her."

"Do you know where she planned to go?"

"No, she just went for a walk with Mr. Jameson."

The officer shot her an incredulous look.

"You're kidding! She went for a walk in the rain with a killer on the loose? I thought Maggie had more sense than that."

He thought for a minute, then tapped the desk.

"Keep trying to get her on the radio. I'll round up the others and start a search for Mickey Stanford, and for Maggie. Forrestville is a small town. It shouldn't be too hard to find her."

Maggie's hand made a slight twitch toward the gun hidden under her raincoat. Mickey's leering grin widened.

"Got the drop on you, didn't I? Suppose you reach under that pretty little coat and hand me that gun. Don't try anything funny or I'll shoot your boyfriend here."

Gritting her teeth in frustration, Maggie removed the pistol and laid it on the ground. Instead of moving it toward Mickey, however, she used her foot to slide it in the opposite direction.

Mickey's grin disappeared, and an expression of pure malice transformed his face into a hideous mask.

"Maggie Jones, you ruined my life! And now I'm going to ruin yours. I think first I'll kill your boyfriend here. Then I'll kill you. And you can die knowing that your son will die next."

"Mickey Stanford, *I* did not ruin your life. You did that yourself."

"Because of you, I served time in prison! You persuaded my wife to testify against me! You made her tell lies about me!"

"Those were not lies. I saw the bruises you left on her and the terror she had of you. She couldn't wait to get away and start a new life without you using her as a punching bag."

Noah could see Mickey working himself into a frenzy. He was proud of Maggie for standing up to the thug, but he recognized Mickey was about to lose his temper. Noah searched the empty streets for a way to get out of this situation.

Mickey noticed him looking around and jeered.

"There's no one here to help you. I made sure of that before I stepped out. You should have picked someone else to be your sweetheart. Because of her, you're going to die."

Noah tried to step in front of Maggie. She shifted her weight and looked up at him, giving her head a slight shake. When she rolled her eyes toward Mickey and back to him, Noah got the message. As an officer of the law, Maggie felt it was her duty to protect him from harm. But as someone who loved her, he wanted to be the one to do the protecting.

Then, behind Mickey, Noah noticed a small figure coming down the street.

Robert!

Chapter 18

Robert bowed as he bid his martial arts instructors goodbye.

"I'll see you Saturday, Sensei Kennedy. Bye Sensei Stephen and Sensei Esther!"

As he turned and headed down the street, it was all he could do to not skip like a five-year-old. Next week he would take his test for junior black belt. Robert was so excited he thought he might burst.

He still had nightmares the first couple of nights after the kidnapping and rescue, but his mom had found a nice lady at the church that did counseling. Mrs. Lewis let him talk and tell her anything he was thinking. Then she helped him figure out ways to handle the fear that still haunted him.

His mother wanted him to keep Bear with him at all times until they could find and apprehend Mickey, but Robert didn't mind. Bear was his buddy, and he was glad to have him along.

He held his bo in one hand and pulled the hood of his raincoat over his head with the other. Bear stayed right by his side even when he put the leash down to adjust the bo and the raincoat.

As Robert neared the alley, he saw three adults ahead

of him. His mother and father faced him, their faces grim and worried. The other adult had his back to him, and it took a moment for Robert to recognize him.

Mickey!

Bear growled and pulled on the leash. Robert stopped and backed away, pulling on the big dog. He knelt next to the Rottweiler and whispered in his ear.

"No, Bear. We have to be smart about this. Look, he's waving a gun around. If we go running up there, he'll just shoot us all."

Robert understood his parents were trying to keep Mickey's attention away from him. He bowed his head and prayed in a frantic whisper.

"Please, God, help! What do I do?"

As soon as he finished praying, an idea came to him. He looked at the long stick in his hand. Robert's mother and his martial arts teachers had drilled him on what to do if threatened by someone with a gun or if he saw someone else threatened.

"Don't hit or kick the gun out of their hands," he remembered. *"That could make the gun go off."*

But he could use the bo as a distraction to give his mother or father the chance to take the man down.

Robert tied the leash around a concrete pillar and commanded Bear to sit. The big dog whined, but obeyed. He focused his eyes on the man threatening Maggie and Noah. Robert knew if he gave the command, Bear would attack. But he feared Mickey would just shoot the dog, then his parents, then him. He watched Bear mouth the leash and hoped he wouldn't chew through it before his parents could capture Mickey.

He commanded the dog to stay, then picked up the bo and approached the trio of adults with stealthy steps.

When he was close enough, Robert threw the long stick
with all his might so that it landed a few feet to the right
of Mickey.

Now it was up to his parents to use the distraction.

Maggie watched her son approach. When she first
noticed him, she thought her heart would stop until she
saw him back away. She glanced at Noah and knew that
he saw Robert, too. They had to keep Mickey's attention
on them and away from who was behind him. What she
had in mind could get them both shot, but she had to try.
So, she started in on Mickey.

"You are nothing but a drug-dealing, wife-beating
thug."

When Mickey growled at her, Maggie continued.

"But, you know what? You don't have to stay that way.
God loves you, Mickey Stanford. He sent His Son to die on
the cross for your sins. If you will admit to God you are a
sinner, believe that Jesus is God's Son who died for your
sins, and commit your life to Him, He will save you from
this life and give you a new, abundant life."

Mickey hesitated for a moment and even looked as if
he was considering her words. Then he sneered and lifted
the gun to point it in her face.

"Don't try that phony religious stuff on me! It don't
do anyone any good!"

Maggie gave him a steady look, though her heart was
hammering so hard she felt sure they could all hear it.

"I'm not talking about religion, Mickey. I'm talking
about a relationship with God."

"Shut up! I don't want to hear any more. It's time for
you to die!"

As he spoke, a long stick came hurtling through the air and landed a few feet from Mickey. He turned and fired his gun toward the sound. Maggie threw herself at him, knocking him to the ground. She rolled onto his arm and grabbed his hand to turn the gun away. Noah piled on top of Mickey to help hold him down.

While Mickey struggled and cursed, Maggie pried his fingers off the pistol. She stood with the gun in her hand and pointed it at the man who tried to kill her.

"Noah, get up and move away from him. Mickey, if you move, I will put a bullet in you."

Maggie's voice was cold and hard. She struggled with the almost overwhelming temptation to just shoot the man and be done with it. Save the state the cost of a trial. As these thoughts ran through her head, Maggie felt a stirring within her heart.

Forgive as God forgave you.

Maggie didn't move, but a battle raged inside her.

"Lord, he is an evil, wicked man who hurt my son. I don't want to forgive him."

They hurt My Son too. He forgave them and He forgave you.

She knew what she had to do, though it warred against everything inside her.

"Yes, Lord. I'll forgive, but it isn't easy."

Maggie knew God didn't ask her to do what was easy. He just wanted her to obey. She reached for her radio and pressed the button to call the station. There was no sound, not even static. Maggie sighed. Of course, the radio would go out now. With her eyes still on Mickey, she called out to her son.

"Robert, go back to the dojo and ask Sensei Esther to call the station."

The boy turned and ran down the street to obey his mother.

Mickey stared at the pistol in Maggie's hand.

"You... you can't shoot me. I'm unarmed and you're an officer of the law."

Though Maggie kept the pistol aimed at him, Mickey stood and inched backward, his eyes on the gun in Maggie's hand. Maggie said nothing else as she watched him, an amused smile spreading across her face. The thug continued to move away from her, his own face relaxing into a smug smirk. He stopped and laughed, his coarse voice grating.

"I don't believe you'll shoot me."

With that, Mickey turned to flee and found himself face to face with Bear. The dog's new leash flapped in the fresh breeze, the ends ragged where he chewed through. Long sharp teeth gleamed in the weak sunshine breaking through the clouds, and an ominous rumble sounded from the big dog as he snarled at the man who hurt his boy.

Mickey stumbled back and almost collided with Maggie, who grabbed his arm, pulling it behind him. She reached for the cuffs dangling from her belt and clicked them on his wrists.

"Mickey Stanford, you're under arrest for kidnapping and attempted murder."

She turned him around and looked him in the eye.

"You ruined your own life, Mickey. Don't blame someone else for the consequences of your own actions."

Chapter 19

Maggie laid her Bible next to her on the pew, then smoothed her dress as she settled in. This was the first time in a long time that she had worn a dress to church. She wore her uniform on most Sundays, believing that the citizens of Forrestville needed to know she was ready for action even on a day off. But today was special. She wanted to look her best.

Rather than wearing her long blond hair in its usual French braid today, Maggie chose to wear it clipped back with a jeweled clasp and flowing over her shoulders. She wore a simple royal blue dress that accentuated the blue in her eyes, and her favorite sapphire necklace and earring set.

Maggie smiled down at Robert, who sat on the other side of her Bible. The pastor had asked that families sit together for this Sunday before Thanksgiving. With all they'd been through the previous week, Robert was glad to comply. He still hovered protectively around his mother with their roles switched since he saved her life.

"Please stand and join me in a song of thanksgiving."

The congregation stood and sang the familiar hymn with gusto. Maggie's heart stirred in gratitude. The words of thanks and praise meant even more to her now.

"May I join you?"

She looked up into the green eyes of the man she had fallen in love with again. A smile spread across her face as she stepped down to make room for Noah. She showed him the song in the hymnal, but continued to hold the song book and share it rather than handing it to Noah and picking up another one.

When he joined his voice with hers in thanking God for His blessings, Maggie's eyes moistened with happiness. She ducked her head for a moment to get the tears under control. When she looked up, Noah gave her an understanding smile.

After the singing, the congregation sat to listen to the pastor, and Noah draped his arm along the back of the pew, his fingers occasionally brushing Maggie's shoulder. Though she tried to pay attention to the sermon, Noah's touch distracted her. More than once Maggie found her attention straying to the man beside her.

When the service ended, she turned to him and put out a hand to stop him from leaving.

"Noah, would you like to join us for lunch?"

His eyes lit up as he studied her face. Her heart beat a little faster as she waited for his answer. His dimple flashed when he spoke.

"I'd love to. Do you want me to bring anything?"

"Just yourself."

Did she sound a little breathless when she answered?

"Maggie, that was a delicious lunch! Thank you for inviting me."

Noah's hands trembled, and he hid them in his lap. He needed to get Maggie alone to find out where they stood. Before Mickey accosted them, Maggie had told him she forgave him and wanted him to have a part in Robert's life. They had not had the chance to discuss if she wanted him to have a part in her life as well.

"Mom, I'll do the dishes."

Maggie and Noah turned to Robert with surprise. Like any normal twelve-year-old, he tried to avoid dish duty as much as possible. So it was unusual for him to volunteer to clean up.

Noah studied his son and thought he saw a twinkle in the boy's eyes. He wondered how much Robert saw and understood. Maybe more than they gave him credit for.

"Maggie, would you like to take a walk? It's nice outside."

Maggie agreed, and they pulled on their jackets.

"Robert, make sure you…"

"I know, Mom, scrape the food into the trash, rinse the dishes well before putting them in the dishwasher, wipe the counters, and take out the trash. Don't worry, I've got this."

Noah smiled. He could understand Maggie's doubts. He remembered what he was like at Robert's age and how he would "wash" dishes. But this time with Maggie was too important to allow something like dirty dishes to distract her.

"Come on, Maggie. He's a smart kid. He'll do it right."

They stepped out into the bright sunshine. It was a beautiful fall day, with just the right amount of crisp coolness in the air. Noah reached out and took Maggie's hand, marveling that she allowed it, but enjoying how their hands still seemed to fit together so well.

As they strolled down the street, Noah couldn't stop stealing glances at Maggie. He knew she watched him as well, and he hoped the attraction was mutual. Her eyes seemed to light up when he stopped next to her at the worship service. And she had shared her hymnal with him, instead of handing it to him and moving away like she did when he first appeared at her church.

"So, when do you have to go back to Shreveport?"

A nervous thrill shot through him. Noah hoped Maggie would like his news, but he still wasn't sure where he stood with her.

"Tomorrow."

"Oh."

Was that disappointment in her voice?

"But I'll be back on Tuesday."

Maggie stopped and stared at him, confusion on her expressive face. Noah found the words tumbling out.

"It seemed better for me to move here to be close to you and Robert, so I bought the old Boyd accounting firm. I'm setting up my own business here. Is that okay with you?"

His heart thundered as he waited for her response. When he saw the big smile on her face, the relief made him wilt.

"That's great, Noah! We need an accounting firm here. And I know Robert will be glad to have you close enough to see every day."

Noah wanted to ask her how she felt, but hesitated. Instead, he changed the subject.

"I talked to Cy this morning. He said Zach has checked into Christ First Rehab and seems to be settling in. Even though Zach hasn't been on drugs, Cy thinks he needs help in making better choices."

"I'd say checking into the rehab is a good first step."

They walked in silence for a moment, both remembering the events of the past few weeks. Gratitude overwhelmed Noah as he gazed down at Maggie's blond head. He had come so close to losing her and Robert, he still woke up at night with his heart pounding at the memory of Mickey threatening her with that pistol.

They circled the block, chatting about his new business and where he would live. When they headed back toward the house, Noah's heart sank in dismay. He wasn't ready to go in the house yet. The sight of the gate to the backyard gave him an idea.

"Maggie, it's too nice outside to go back into the house. Can we go to the backyard and sit in the swing for a while?"

He held his breath, hoping she would agree. Maggie stopped and took a deep breath of the autumn air, then nodded.

"I like that idea. Let's go."

Maggie opened the gate and led him to the swing. When he sat down, she pushed with her foot to move the swing in a gentle, gliding motion. Noah tried to get his thoughts in order and use the speech he had practiced. Nothing came out. Finally, he abandoned the speech and simply opened his mouth.

"Maggie, do you remember what I asked you before Mickey, uh, interrupted?"

She blushed as she nodded.

"I've been thinking about that."

Noah's stomach cramped with an attack of nerves. He was afraid to find out what she had been thinking, yet he knew it was the most important thing anyone would ever say to him.

He turned to Maggie and took her hands in his, studying her as if he could see her answer on her face or in her beautiful sapphire eyes.

"What did you decide?"

He held his breath. Her answer was almost too low for him to hear.

"I want you to be part of my life, too."

"Really?"

Maggie smiled, a big beautiful smile that showed her even white teeth. She reached up to caress his jaw.

"Really."

Noah leaned forward, his lips hovering just above hers as if giving her chance to pull away. Maggie leaned toward him and met his lips with her own. The kiss deepened, and he pulled her into his arms. After the kiss, they sat in silence, content to hold each other.

A few moments later, they heard a muted cheer from behind them. They turned to see Robert and Bear standing by the window, watching them. Robert wore a huge grin on his face as he gave them a thumbs up before turning away and disappearing down the hallway.

"That boy!"

Maggie and Noah burst out laughing and stood to go in. He reached and pulled her back into his arms, looking down into her sweet face.

"Maggie, you asked me to forgive you that day. I want you to know that I not only forgive you, I love you with all my heart."

"Noah, I love you too. I think I never stopped, but the anger and hurt blocked it. Once God helped me to forgive you, the love grew again. Now, I can't imagine my life without you. I don't want to imagine my life without you."

Noah kissed her again.

Chapter 20

"You may kiss the bride."

Noah released Maggie's hands and reached to cup her head, drawing her close and touching his lips to hers. Maggie wound her arms around his neck and pulled him closer, deepening the kiss. A whistle erupted from the back of the church, and a wave of laughter followed.

Robert stood near his parents, his face red with embarrassment and pleasure. He grinned at the crowd as they waited for the newlyweds to finish their long embrace.

"You ready?"

Noah's voice was a husky growl as his eyes drank in the sight of his wife. Maggie blushed at the look in his eyes. She ran one finger down his jaw, then took his hand and turned to face the crowd in the church. The pastor stood waiting for them with a grin. He cleared his throat and addressed the guests.

"Ladies and gentlemen, may I present to you Mr. and Mrs. Noah Jameson."

Maggie and Noah stood near the glistening wedding cake, admiring it."

"I almost hate to cut it, it's so pretty," Maggie laughed. "Linda, you did a terrific job! Thank you!"

Robert had to agree, though the bakery owner only blushed and waved a dismissive hand before returning to her table. The boy wondered why she blushed at the compliment. He turned back to the wedding cake in time to see his parents join hands and send the blade on the decorated knife slicing through the white frosting with blue and purple roses.

Maggie had told him he could serve the cake once they got their pieces, and he could hardly wait. Robert loved playing host and handing out the refreshments. Of course, he wanted a piece of cake for himself. He was almost drooling over it now.

"Hey Robert! How do you like your new dad?"

Robert's friends gathered around the table, wolfing down cake and guzzling punch. They questioned him with curious eyes about if he minded having a stepfather. He simply smiled and offered more cake. After a long discussion with his parents, Robert had decided not to tell the complete story. Noah was his father, and that was enough for him.

"Have I told you how beautiful you are?"

Noah's whisper behind her ear sent a shiver of pleasure through Maggie. She turned to face her new husband and studied him, her intense gaze boring into his eyes. He fidgeted as he returned her gaze in confusion and a hint of alarm.

"What? Did I say something wrong?"

Maggie stared at him in silence for another long moment before giving Noah a tender smile. She reached to caress his jaw.

"No, I only wanted to admire the man I just married. I feel like I've known you all my life, and yet…"

She struggled with tears and Noah enfolded her in his arms and held her. He kissed the top of her head and waited for her.

"And yet what?"

"And yet, you are a new man. You are so different from the man I met and married twenty years ago."

"Yes, and I am very different from the man you left thirteen years ago."

Maggie stepped back and dabbed the tears from the corner of her eye. She sent a reassuring smile toward David and Christy, who watched with concern from across the room. When Noah reached for her hand, she interlaced her fingers with his.

"Yes, you are most definitely different from the man I left. I can see God's handiwork in your life and I am so proud and happy to see the godly man you have become."

Noah pulled her close again and ran his finger down her cheek.

"My prayer is that I will get it right this time, Maggie. I want to love you and Robert the way I should have done back then."

Maggie laid her finger on his lips.

"No regrets," she whispered. "From this day forward we will be the couple and the family God wants us to be. He has forgiven us and we have forgiven each other. No more looking back, right?"

Noah touched his lips to hers.

"No more looking back."

Dear Reader,

Thank you for reading *Unintended Target*. In this story Maggie and Robert both have to learn to forgive others while Noah has to learn to let go of the shame and regret that cling to him.

Noah finds salvation in Christ while in jail and breaks free from the alcohol and drugs with the help of his friend, Cy, and Christ First Rehab. He's made amends to *almost* everyone – except Maggie. That one just seems too hard. When Noah finds an article about her in the newspaper, he knows it's time and drives to Forrestville to seek her out.

Maggie has a hard time letting go of the past and learning to trust Noah. She doesn't want him to hurt Robert - or her. Noah is frustrated with Maggie's distrust, but he hangs in there and shows her that he *has* changed from an addict to a godly man. It takes an attack, a kidnapping, and a rescue to show Maggie the kind of man her ex-husband has grown into.

Forgiving someone who has hurt you is hard. Forgiving someone who has hurt someone you love is even harder. I hope this book has not only entertained, but also encouraged you if you need to forgive someone who hurt you, or even need to forgive yourself.

Can I ask a favor from you? Would you post a review on Amazon or Goodreads about the book? I want to know what you liked and what you didn't like. That's how I learn so I can write books that you will want to read over and over.

I love to hear from my readers! You can contact me at tina@tinamiddleton.net

You can also follow me on:

Facebook:
https://www.facebook.com/tinaann.middleton/

Twitter:
https://twitter.com/mid_tina

Goodreads:
https://www.goodreads.com/author/show/17729966.
Tina_Middleton

Amazon:
https://www.amazon.com/Tina-Middle-
ton/e/B0821W1T9S?ref=sr_ntt_srch_
lnk_1&qid=1637428687&sr=1-1

I also have a YouTube channel for new writers and
those who want to be writers. Check it out at https://
www.youtube.com/channel/UCWHX8rNgqsM5wMnf-
bX6IWZQ/featured

Turn the page for a sneak peek at the prologue for
Wounded Target.

May God bless you richly!
Tina Ann Middleton

The Forrestville Series
Book Four

Tina Ann Middleton

**Shield
Of
Faith**

Publishing

Prologue

*S*weat beaded, then dripped down the side of Mark's face as the sun baked him. Long sleeves and forty pounds of equipment, though necessary, did not help him stay cool in this desert climate. A light breeze provided a brief respite from the stifling heat.

Mark and the small group of soldiers with him drew closer to a bombed-out village. Intel had indicated the presence of a pocket of insurgents that were terrorizing the area. The first priority was to find them; second priority was to take them out.

A shell screamed overhead and landed about fifteen yards from them. Mark shared a glance with his buddy, John Miller, apprehension darkening his hazel eyes.

"That one came a little too close."

John nodded as he wiped the sweat off his forehead, then adjusted his helmet and pulled the rifle strap higher on his shoulder.

"Yeah. We need to find a place to hunker down and check things out."

The commander called to his troops and motioned to a nearby shack that leaned to one side, loose boards creaking. A wave of claustrophobia swept over Mark at the thought of all twelve of them packed into that building. If it fell on top of them...

The unit's dog, Shadow, trotted in front of them. As they neared the dubious shelter, the Belgian Malinois crouched and growled, the fur rising on her neck as her ears swiveled forward. Sergeant Strong waved the group back and they retreated from the structure as a burst of gunfire surrounded them.

Amid shouts and screams, Mark crouched and swept the area with his eyes. A figure stood a few yards from him; dark eyes glittering with hate as he aimed his gun at Mark.

Instinct and training caused Mark to pull the trigger on his own weapon. The man fell, but before Mark could move a sharp pain pierced his left shoulder. He flinched and looked down. Blood spread in a circle on his shirt, but Mark felt detached from the idea he'd been shot. He heard John's voice as if from far away.

"Mark, c'mon! Sarge says to retreat. We have to get out of here! Let's go!"

Mark moved his head to get a glimpse of his friend; his motions slow and clumsy.

"I'm hit."

John's arm came around his shoulders to turn him around.

"Yeah, buddy, I know. We'll get you some help after we get outta here!"

John released his shoulders and took a firm grip of Mark's arm, tugging him away from the action. Mark tried to make his feet move, but he felt as if he was moving through molasses. Another spray of gunfire separated the men. Darkness edged Mark's vision as he searched for his friend. When he saw John, his stomach spasmed with nausea.

His buddy's head and chest spurted blood from large holes. The vacant, unseeing eyes told Mark that John was gone, but he felt for a pulse anyway. Pain and disbelief rooted his feet to the desert floor even as the firefight raged around him.

The sensation of a cold nose startled Mark and he looked down to find Shadow nudging and pulling on his hand in an effort to move him to safety.

"I'm coming, Shadow."

Mark knelt and lifted John onto his shoulder in a fireman's carry, despite the blood oozing from his own wound and the pain radiating throughout his body. Shadow barked and paced in frantic motions intended to herd him to safety, but he could not leave his best friend laying on enemy soil.

Once he had John settled on his shoulder, Mark tried to run from the scene, but his feet would not move. The Malinois barked again, then yelped as a bullet found its target. Mark turned to find the canine who had come to save his life, but the animal was stretched out on the sand, her coat covered in blood. So much blood. It covered the ground, the people. Mark felt it dripping down his chest. A red haze covered his vision.

Mark sat up with a jolt, his heart pounding until he thought he would be sick. He shoved aside the damp sheets and swung his feet to the floor.

Come on. Deep breaths. In through the nose, out through the mouth.

He coached himself until his heart rate slowed and he felt he could stand without passing out or throwing up. Mark stood and walked to the bathroom, holding on to the furniture for stability. He filled a glass with water and drained it, then closed the toilet lid and slumped onto the cold porcelain.

The dreams were coming more often, especially when

he was tired or stressed. But he was fine. There were others who were much worse off than him, he told himself.

He was fine. He had to be.

Made in the USA
Middletown, DE
16 November 2023

42886806R00128